MY

YEAR

IN

THE

MIDDLE

MY YEAR IN THE MIDDLE

Lila Quintero Weaver

SCHOLASTIC INC.

No part of this publication may be reproduced, stored in a retrieval system, or transmitted in any form or by any means, electronic, mechanical, photocopying, recording, or otherwise, without written permission of the publisher. For information regarding permission, write to Candlewick Press, 99 Dover Street, Somerville, MA 02144.

ISBN 978-1-338-61072-7

12 11 10 9   21 22 23 24

Printed in the U.S.A.   40

First Scholastic printing, September 2019

This book was typeset in Berling.

To Paul, Jude, Benjamin, and Caitlin—
with love and fierce devotion.

★1★
THANK YOU, MADELINE MANNING

Everybody in gym class is talking. We're like a chicken house with thirty biddies going *cheep-cheep-cheep* all at once. It's Monday, April 20, 1970—a fine, sunny afternoon in Red Grove, Alabama. We've just finished six weeks of volleyball, and everybody thinks we're coasting easy to the end of school.

But with three short blasts of her mighty whistle, Mrs. Underwood, who's feared and famous for push-up marathons and killer jump-rope sessions, calls for quiet.

"Y'all hush your yakking and listen up. We're doing something new today." She plants her feet in a wide stance and crosses those beefy arms of hers. You can feel it; she's about to drop a bomb. She's got that saucy look on her face that you might see on a tomcat circling a canary's cage. "Girls, there's six weeks left till Field Day, when busloads of whippersnappers from County show up for competitions. Time to get y'all good and ready." A murmur starts up. County is a bigger school than ours, and it's full of toughies, or so we hear. "That's why today you'll run the whole kit and caboodle." She waves her paw in the shape of the driveway we're standing on, which circles Red Grove Elementary *and* the high school. It's about a bazillion times farther than we've ever run before.

There's a second of stunned silence.

"Y'all got that or do you need me to spell it?"

The class erupts.

"All the way around? You can't be serious!"

"Indeed I am," she says.

"But that's too far!"

"Too far?" she hoots. "You lazy sheilas wouldn't know 'far' if it walked up on legs."

"But I'm not running at Field Day," one girl says. "I'm doing Hula-Hoops!"

"I'm doing horseshoes," somebody else says.

"Wheelbarrow races," another girl whines.

The biddies are all atwitter. Mrs. Underwood blasts the whistle and yells, "Shaddup!" Everybody gets quiet. She whips off her sunglasses and stares us down. She's solid built. Her shorts come down to the tops of her muscular knees. She wears a floppy fisherman's hat without the fish lures and a safari-style shirt with pockets everywhere. She's a sight.

Then she speaks in a near-whisper we've come to dread. "You poor little babies. You have such a hard life. I feel so sorry for you." But you can tell she doesn't feel sorry for anybody, least of all a bunch of whiny sixth-grade girls.

I scan the crowd. Nearly every face is miserable—even Abigail Farrow's. Abigail has been my best friend since fifth grade, when she and her widowed father moved up here from Florida. "Lu," she whispers, her mouth in an upside-down *U,* "don't you hate this? And we're stuck with her for *six more years*!"

Funny thing is, I *don't* hate this. Normally, I'm scared to pieces of Mrs. Underwood, but right this minute something strange is brewing. The notion of running this driveway has my attention. This is big. This is real. Not like those easy-peasy kindergarten races we've done up to now.

One other girl is calm as a sheet of glass: Belinda Gresham. Out of the corner of my eye, I see her doing neck rolls and warm-ups, shaking one foot, then the other, back and forth.

Belinda's all right, from what little I know of her. Half the time she's hiding behind a book. The other half, she's cutting up with her friends, Angie and Willa. They're some of

3

the newish girls who transferred to Red Grove Elementary at the start of sixth grade. That's when public schools were finally integrated. Before that, we had no black students. Not a one. And neither did the high school. Plenty of white folks wish it had stayed that way, and here lately, some families have started sending their kids to a whites-only private school called East Lake Academy.

Mrs. Underwood runs a piece of chalk across the driveway, leaving behind a rough white mark. Three blasts of her whistle and we line up. We're at the west end of the driveway, behind the high-school gym that they let us elementary kids use and not too far from the baseball fields. A boys' PE class is out there. You can hear aluminum bats going *ping, ping* and voices calling out, "I got it! I got it!"

Mrs. Underwood backs out of the way and bellows, "Ready, ladies? On the count of three." You can feel everybody tense up. "One, two, three!" Her whistle blasts, and we take off like a wild herd stampeding down the pavement. A huge group of girls moves out at top speed, the way you would for a hundred-yard dash. Belinda is up there, tearing through to the front in no time.

But this is no hundred-yard dash. They're making a mistake going out so fast. Me, I start off at a steady rhythm. You've got to save something for the distance. I figured this out when I was ten, from watching the 1968 Olympics. Although it took some doing to adjust the antenna on our dinky TV, Papá and I burned up hours huddled in front of the track-and-field events. We went cuckoo cheering for the Americans, even though the four of us Oliveras—Mamá, Papá, Marina, and I—are from Argentina. We moved up here when I was little.

Mamá tried her best to hush us. "¡Por favor, cállense!" She said that any minute the neighbors were going to complain, and what was she supposed to tell them? Papá said let them complain because we live in the United States now and we *are* Americans, so we should cheer for Americans, and do it at the top of our lungs. End of story.

There were good and plenty Americans to cheer for: javelin throwers, long jumpers, high jumpers, shot-putters, and pole-vaulters. But we went nutsiest for the track people. That Madeline Manning was something else. She ran the eight hundred meters for the United States, and I couldn't take my eyes off her. A little voice told me, "Study up, Lu." The next day, I cut her picture out of the sports pages and stuck it in an old cigar box I keep under my bed.

Here's what I noticed: the Olympians ran with smooth, long strides and calm faces, like they had everything under control. Papá pointed out that they weren't flapping their feet any old which way or sticking their elbows out like prissy hens. They knew when to cruise and when to turn on the jets. They saved something for the finish.

So out on the school driveway, it's like those Olympic runners are coaching me. Stay smooth. Move your feet quickly, but don't go at top speed sooner than you have to. And don't panic about whoever's far out in front because they'll run out of gas before long.

Why, thank you, Madeline Manning.

★ 2 ★
BLUE BLAZES

One by one, I catch the girls in the middle of the pack. Most of their faces are red and blotchy. No wonder—they bolted like rabbits at the start, and now their tails are dragging.

During a long stretch of pavement with nobody but me running it, I hear yells coming from open windows. *"Go, go, go!"* Are they cheering for me? Most high schoolers treat us elementary squirts like we're invisible. We have to use their cafeteria since we don't have our own. We have to use their gym, including the stinky old locker room, since we don't have that either. We're right there under their noses, and they *still* don't see us. On top of all that, I'm a runt. Turn me loose in the halls of Red Grove High School and I'm like a Chihuahua in a pack of Great Danes.

Right this minute, though, I feel tall. As I fly around the first two curves of the driveway, speed takes over my feet, and it seems like I might launch into the sky. I pass the band room. Tubas, trombones, drums, clarinets, and flutes all blare together like at football games, when every kid screams the fight song and the cheerleaders whip the crowd into a fever. In a flash, I dream up an oval track like the one at the Olympics, with stands full of people going bonkers. *Lu, Lu! Lu—Lu—Lu!* Their feet are like thunder on the bleachers. *Lu, Lu! Lu—Lu—Lu!* I'm pretty sure if this dream ever came true, it would make the sports pages of the *Birmingham Post-Herald*.

I catch up with some of the faster girls and can't help but notice they're spent. Two of them try to stay with me, eyes bulging and teeth clenched, but they've got no kick left. Too bad, bunnies—you're dust. Before long, I start gaining on the lead group. Connie Smith's long brown ponytail swishes back and forth like a windshield wiper. It's news to me that Connie can run this fast. She moved to town only last summer. Still, I manage to pass her, and as soon as I do, I've got a clear shot of Belinda, who's out in front with arms a-pumping to beat the band. She has no idea I'm reeling her in. When I run up alongside her, Belinda's cool-as-a-cat self does a double take, and I can just about read her mind:

Whoa! This little runt? She and I go neck and neck into the last curve.

Straddling the finish line, Mrs. Underwood squints over her sunglasses trying to make out who's leading. By this time, I'm ahead of Belinda by three or four strides. Off to my right, a few boys drag canvas bags full of baseball bats. They stop and watch. Never before have boys cared one whit what I do. My face burns like kingdom come, but I keep running. Faster. Now the chalk line is square in front of me. I watch my feet crossing it, but I don't break stride or slow down till I pass Mrs. Underwood. "Way to go, Olivera!" she hollers as I zoom by.

Belinda's right behind me. Soon, Connie and one of the black girls, Angie, come tearing around the curve, like a couple of long-legged fillies on a racetrack. The four of us are wrung as rags. Connie, who's never said much to me, flops down on the grass, while the rest of us walk in circles, hands on hips, catching our breath.

Angie sasses Belinda. "Girl, you let that peewee beat you?"

"Didn't let her!" Belinda says. "She's the real thing." My ears perk straight up. Nobody has ever called me "the real thing."

Connie rolls over on her stomach and pays us no mind.

Her chin's propped in her hands, and her eyes are locked in a squint. I can't tell if she's staring at the curve to see who's coming next or if she's studying the baseball fields. Every time a bat goes *ping*, sending a ball flying, you can hear the boys clamoring. Seems like Connie cares about *that* more than running.

I wander closer to Belinda, or maybe she wanders closer to me. All I know is that when our eyes meet, she gives me a nod. Respect. I nod back. She deserves respect, too.

"Dang, girl. Where'd you learn to fly?" she says.

"Beats me. That was the first time."

"Uh-uh. Quit joshing me." She fiddles with her ponytail, which she wears off to one side, like an arrow that says, *Here she is: Belinda!* The ponytail's held together with a fancy hickey-ma-doodle that matches her pink nail polish. My Lordy, she's stylish. Me, I'm nowhere close to fancy. But we're both fast, and if Mrs. Underwood puts us to this test again, Belinda's not going down easy.

By and by, the rest of the class arrives. The last group takes forever and a day, and by the time they shuffle around the bend, Mrs. Underwood's all out of patience. "Pick it up, slowpokes! My grandma can run faster than that in steel-toed army boots!" Belinda and I snicker. It's our first time laughing together. Everything's our first. First run, first nod, first talk. My scalp is tingly from all these firsts. Still, I can't forget where I am and who's watching, because around here, black and white kids don't mix. No siree bob.

One girl stumbles to the finish and flops down on the grass, her sides heaving like a minnow out of water. Soon other girls join her on that patch of grass. Not me. It's itchy and crawling with fire ants and chiggers. Phyllis Hartley moans and groans that her lungs are about to explode. Ages ago in fourth grade, Phyllis and I were best friends, but we've barely spoken since Missy Parnell in her matchy outfits took over as Queen of the World. And now, just as somebody mentions that I won the race, my stomach churns when Phyllis blurts out, "What did she do *that* for?"

At long last, here comes Missy, who doesn't even pretend to run. She plops down on the curb next to Phyllis, whips her bouncy hair off her neck with one hand, and fans herself with the other. "I'm burning up, y'all. Flat burning up." Her face looks like an overripe tomato.

Phyllis grabs Missy's arm. "Can you believe Lu won? *Lu!*" That's when Missy shoots me the devil of a look. Mean green eyes in a tomato face.

Good gravy, Phyllis, why did you have to point that out to Missy? Might as well poke an ant pile with a stick. One place I never wanted to be was on Missy's bad side. Lord knows I've done all I could to stay out of it.

Mrs. Underwood says, "Listen up, ladies—I mean,

11

babies—I have good news, and I have bad news. Which do y'all want to hear first?"

Everybody says, "The bad news!"

"The good news is that y'all survived. After I give you the bad news, march yourselves into that locker room, get dressed, and skedaddle your lazy buns to your next class." She holds off until the whispers die down. "The bad news is that you're going to repeat this run tomorrow, the next day, the day after that . . ." An explosion of groans and screams drowns her out. I barely hear the end of Mrs. Underwood's spiel: "And we'll keep it up for these next six weeks until y'all get in shape for Field Day!"

The caterwauling near about busts my eardrums. "Every day?" Some girls look at me scandalized, like I should gnash my teeth, too. But I don't say a dadgum word because here's my secret: I'm happy, happier than anything's made me in a long while. Today I found out that running feels good and winning feels extra good. And now that I've gotten a taste of winning, I'm not going down easy either. No siree.

"Enough whining! Get back inside!" Mrs. Underwood yells. "Hustle, hustle, hustle."

I head for the locker room at a trot. My buddy Abigail slings her arm around my shoulder. "You little speed demon, you made us all look bad out there." Her face is the color of a boiled lobster, but she's grinning. "Proud of you, but don't do it again!"

I'm about to speed off to my next class when Mrs. Underwood collars me. "Holy Toledo, Olivera. You can run like the blue blazes! Never saw that coming! Field Day's gonna be yours!" She grins so wide that her gold molars show.

I grin back. That makes two of us. I never saw it coming either. Never knew I had a motor in these little bird legs of mine.

The Red Grove Gazette

COURTHOUSE BESIEGED
BY NEGRO PROTESTORS

★ 3 ★

SAM

Hurrying along the covered walkway that runs between RGHS and the elementary school, I set out for Miss Garrett's social studies class. I'm floating. "Field Day's gonna be yours," Mrs. Underwood said, and those words still ring in my ears.

I drop my books on the front desk of the middle row. Miss Garrett's classroom is like every other at our school. White kids sit on one side and black kids on the other. I'm one of the few middle-rowers who split the difference, since the four of us don't exactly belong to either group. Most of the white kids come from families that are against integration and don't want to sit anywhere near the black kids. The middle row isn't like that. Our moms and dads believe in equal rights and all that good stuff, which makes us weirdos in some people's eyes. Being a foreigner and all, I'm already sort of weird—kind of like a sparrow thrown in with a bunch of blue jays.

The other kids in the middle row are Sam McCorkle, who sits right behind me; Abigail, who's behind Sam; and Paige, whose dad is a college professor and whose mom, Mrs. Donnelly, is our homeroom and language arts teacher.

Sam glances my way and starts fussing with his fountain pen. Could be he's practicing finger movements for the tuba. I hear he auditioned for the RGHS marching band. I've been noticing him lately. Ever since he got brand-new contact lenses last month, his eyes stay extra wide and he blinks tons more than normal. Turns out Sam's got gray eyes and long lashes. Hello. Never paid attention to his eyes before, and I've known him since *first grade*. Up to now, he's worn thick, old-fogy glasses that shrank his eyes down to BBs. Also, he used to keep his hair in that 1950s military cut that made you want to salute, but not exactly get friendly. Here lately, he's been looking like a regular boy with real eyes and longer hair—not past the collar, though, or Mr. Abrams, the principal, would raise h-e-double-hockey-sticks.

Sam's dad is Red Grove's Presbyterian minister. My sister calls him a hero. I don't remember much because I was only in first grade, but I know that black people in Alabama were marching for their rights, and white people—especially our governor back then, George Wallace—wouldn't budge an inch for them. But the McCorkles were different. They always took the side of the black folks. Grown-ups didn't explain squat to us, so all we knew was that Sam was absent from school for weeks and got his lessons from a home tutor. Later, my sister told me why: because the McCorkles were getting telephoned death threats! They had to call the FBI and everything! Those people who made the phone calls must've figured on scaring Reverend McCorkle off, but he proved them flat wrong and kept right on being brave. Wowee.

★4★

THE ENVELOPE

A vase of pink carnations sits on Miss Garrett's desk, where she always keeps fresh flowers. "Class, please take out your election notebooks and open them to your last entry." I sneak a peek at Belinda, one row to my right. She's fanning herself with a sheet of cardboard, but I don't see a drop of sweat on her.

A half-dozen girls straggle in late. At the head of this line are Missy and Phyllis, my once and sometimes friend. My notebook's already open with yesterday's headline staring back at me: "Candidates to Address Public Friday on TV." Every day we show Miss Garrett that we're keeping up with the governor's primary election, which is two weeks from tomorrow. Ex-governor George Wallace is trying like a house afire to snatch his old job back from the governor we have now, Albert Brewer.

While Miss Garrett moves along row by row, checking students' work, two-thirds of the class chatters away. I see where most of the jibber-jabber's coming from. In their far-right corner, Missy and Phyllis are having a jolly old time. If she were here, Marina would give me a talking-to because that's how sisters are. "Why do you care what they do? You don't belong with them. Get yourself a real friend, one with brains and gumption."

What does she think Abigail is, chopped liver? After Phyllis dropped me like a hot potato for Missy back in fourth grade, I had to twiddle my thumbs till Abigail moved up here so I could get myself one good, solid friend. But I still wish Phyllis would be nice to me again. Sure, I'd like to make Marina proud, so I mostly pretend not to give a plug nickel what Phyllis thinks about me, but it seems like my eyes have a mind of their own today.

A kid nicknamed Spider has his hand up. "Hey, Miss Garrett!" His uncle owns the black radio station in town, and every afternoon he lets Spider man the microphone for an hour, playing hits and taking special requests. You won't find a kid in the whole county, black or white, who doesn't recognize his voice. "Miss Garrett, how come you didn't say anything when you looked at my notebook?" he says. Kids giggle. "You told Charles, 'very good.'"

Charles jumps in now. "Because mine's very good and yours ain't, pea brain."

Everybody hoots, but that's just Charles cutting up. Spider's no pea brain; he's the number-one math whiz in the sixth grade.

On the white side of the room, the girls in the corner are busy sorting and shuffling papers. Missy whispers in Phyllis's ear. Phyllis grabs a pen, scribbles, and hands a small stack of papers to Nick Flynn, the boy in front of her. He passes the stack to the next person. These must be the invitations for Phyllis's birthday party. My stomach does a cartwheel. I've been to every party of hers since first grade—surely she won't leave me out in the cold. But after the way she acted in today's gym class, who can say?

All the talking forces Miss Garrett to run for the light switch. She flips the lights off and on, off and on. "Quieeeeeeet!"

I feel a tap on my shoulder. It's Sam. His eyes go blink-blink, and he silently hands me an envelope. I see he's got one, too. I stick mine in my book bag real quick before Miss Garrett can notice. You can't be too careful. Lots of teachers catch a note and make you stand up and read it aloud.

As Nick passes invitations to the next kid, a loose piece of paper slides off his desk and skids across the floor, past my desk, to the black side of the room, where Charles snatches it up. "Oo-wee, looky here!" He reads it aloud: "Governor George Wallace Is Coming to Red Grove Friday, May First! Family-Friendly Gathering! Fun and Games for All Ages!" A few kids bust out laughing because Charles is using his fake grown-up voice.

Then Charles starts up a rhyme: "Georgie Porgy, puddin' and pies. Kissin' on babies and telling big lies." Now nearly everybody laughs.

But Nick, whose dad is the head honcho of the local Wallace campaign, isn't having it. "Better shut your fat mouth, if you know what's good for you."

"You shut *your* fat mouth," Charles says, and shoves the flyer across the middle row, back in Nick's direction.

"Boys, settle back down," Miss Garrett says. She tells us to turn in our books to chapter twelve, page one hundred and thirty-five.

When the last bell of the day rings, Sam taps me on the shoulder again. "Hey, are you going to Phyllis's party?"

Is my jaw unhinged? Silent Sam is speaking to me for the first time in all his born days! I doubt he's ever spoken much to *any* girl. And since talking to boys is nothing *I* ever do on purpose, I just blurt, "Guess so," and then I've got to haul it to the boarding zone to catch my bus.

★5★
BUS 18

The bus is crowded, and three of us end up sharing a two-seater, right behind Ricky Hughes. He's a big seventh-grader whose favorite things in life are yanking girls' ponytails and giving wedgies to smaller boys. My seatmates are eighth-grade girls who run their mouths constantly. Ricky keeps turning around to smart off at them, and they smart off right back.

It's stuffy, and I slide the window open to the halfway point. Below us, a passel of kids mill around, waiting to board their buses. I think Belinda rides a bus, too. My eyes rove back and forth, hoping to spy a bright-pink hickey-ma-doodle attached to a sideways ponytail. A clump of high-school guys wearing dashikis stand around, most of them with picks that jut straight out of their Afro haircuts. Mr. Abrams won't stand for that. "Stick that thing in your pocket before I haul you to the office!"

I feel a jab in my left side. "Hey, didn't I see you running in fifth period?" the girl next to me says. Her name is Denise.

"You were watching?"

"Sure, me and the whole typing class was at the window cheering!" I near about choke. A class full of eighth-graders cheered for *me*?

Ricky whirls around to face me with a smirk. "Ever heard of Tina Briggs?"

"Nope."

The girl by the aisle says, "Ricky Hughes, why don't you mind your own beeswax?"

"This *is* my own beeswax. Tina Briggs is my cousin. She goes to County, and she just came in third in the state track meet. *Third*." He points a stubby finger inches from my nose. "You ought to write her name down because she's gonna whip the tar out of you at Field Day."

Denise snorts. "You lie like a dog! Your cousin is a *nobody*."

"She is not!"

"She is too!"

I shrink back in my seat. As soon as the words *state track meet* rolled off his tongue, my pulse meter went *tickety-tick-tick-tack*. Tina Briggs? Even her name sounds fast.

The bus swings out of the boarding zone and onto the school driveway. *Pop.* Somebody shoots a rubber band across the aisle. I've never paid this driveway a lick of attention, but now every detail jumps out. Over there's the big pothole I dodged. There's the patch of crabgrass next to the lunchroom. Right there's where I passed Connie. And here's the teachers' parking lot, where Miss Garrett's blue Monte Carlo shines brightest of all.

Thinking about Miss Garrett reminds me of Phyllis's party invitation. I fumble around in my book bag until my hand lands on a corner of the envelope. I tear it open and pull out the card inside—but it's blank. It's just a plain white index card. Huh? I turn the card over, and there's nothing more to see. No balloons, no party hats, no "You're Invited." I flip it back again, wondering what in tarnation I missed. Where's the invitation?

"Oh, Lordy," Denise says. "Please tell me you're not about to be sick. You're looking mighty green."

"No, I just . . ." I peek in the envelope again, in case I've lost my marbles. "There's supposed to be an invitation in here."

"Let me see." She takes hold of the index card and peers

at the front and back, just like I did. "This isn't no invitation, not in my book. Hand me that envelope." She looks at the front of the envelope and lets out a long whistle. "Somebody doesn't like you."

I look at the envelope, too, and that's when I almost faint dead away. There, in Phyllis's handwriting, it says "Loser Olivera." *Loser?* Phyllis knows good and well how to spell Luisa, my given name. She's just being mean.

No, this is Missy's doing. *She* made Phyllis write that.

Now I'm glummer than glum. Rubber bands zing past my head, and I barely flinch.

A knot of worry has me by the throat, and it's getting bigger by the minute. As we round the last curve before the street, the spot where I passed Belinda reminds me how easy my running felt, kind of like floating on a breeze. There I was, believing I was somebody, but now all kinds of darts are zigzagging back and forth inside my head.

★6★
THE PLAYGROUND

By the time I get home, I'm itching like fire to talk to Abigail about the invitation. I figure she'll know what to do because that's how she is. But does Abigail answer her phone? Nope. I try over and over.

As usual, Mamá's in the dining room at her sewing machine. "Lu, why are you making so many calls?" she says.

"No reason." One thing's for sure, you can't sneak a phone call in this house. The sound of the dial rotating echoes all over.

I drag the cigar box out from under my bed and find that 1968 newspaper clipping about Madeline Manning. It's yellow now and kind of ragged around the edges, but in the photo, you can still see her big smile and the Olympic gold medal shining in the sun.

I thumbtack the article slapdab in the middle of the corkboard that hangs over my dresser. Now the first thing that will greet me every morning will be Madeline Manning's face.

I go clean through my homework assignments and read nine pages of Archie comics before Abigail calls. She's been at a yearbook staff meeting. "Want to ride bikes?"

"Shoot, yeah. Let me go ask my mom."

Mamá sews wedding dresses for people around town, and right now, a big wedding is taking up every waking minute. I've figured out something: when Mamá's sewing is humming along, getting permission from her is a piece of cake. But if she's having problems, forget it. Today, things are going hunky-dory, so after Mamá gives me her okay, I ask my sister if I can borrow her ten-speed bike, and Marina, who's been chained to the typewriter writing college papers since she was born, just nods yes without even looking up.

Abigail and I always meet at the corner of Greene and Early. We usually ride bikes in that neighborhood and end up at the park playground. She's already at our meeting spot, riding in lazy circles around the empty intersection when I get there. By the time we reach the playground, she's pink-faced and huffing. We park our bikes by the fence and slip through the unlocked gate. Nobody's here but us.

I tell her about the invitation. "Even if we're not best buddies anymore, why would Phyllis think I'm a *loser*?"

Abigail doesn't act the least bit worried. "Did you call her?"

"Heck, no. I'd be too embarrassed."

"Why? What's the big deal?"

"Because of Missy. She told Phyllis to swap out the invitation. I saw them whispering."

"Why would she do that?"

"She hates my guts."

"Since when?"

"Since today at PE." I pause. "Not that Missy's ever liked me much, but at least she's never acted this snotty to me."

"Lu, come on! You're sooo paranoid!" Abigail plunks herself down into a swing and sits there, laughing.

I claim a swing next to hers. "You should've seen how she looked at me after the run. Like she wanted to kill me."

"So what? She wants to kill lots of people. She's like that, and you can't do a blessed thing about it."

"But now I don't know if I'm invited or not!"

"You are! Stop worrying!" she says. "I'll talk to Phyllis for you. I bet she'll give you a new invitation."

"Hope so."

I wanted to ask her about Sam, too, and why he wondered if I was going to the party. Abigail understands boys way better than I do, so maybe she can figure out what he was thinking. But before I can bring it up, she starts begging me to go to that Wallace rally with her, the one advertised on Nick's flyer. "Daddy will drive us. It's going to be a blast. There's going to be a cakewalk and prizes and stuff. And everybody will be there. Positively everybody."

"A cakewalk? What the heck is that?"

"It's a game, kind of like musical chairs," she says. "Well, not exactly like musical chairs, but still, it's loads of fun, and the prizes are cakes."

That sounds pretty fun to me, but I'm still not sure. "What about Wallace? My sister would kill me dead if she found out I went to his rally. My family's for Brewer."

"So are we! But don't worry, because my dad said you can spend the night. That way, your folks won't even know you went."

"Well . . . I guess it's okay."

"Goody!" She digs her toes into the dirt and shoves off backward. Pretty soon I'm up in the air, too, sailing clear above the packed earth of the playground. Our swings go *creak whine, creak whine*.

After a while, we hear voices. Past the trees, two boys coast along on bikes. When they roll through the gate and inside the playground, I see that it's Sam and his little brother, Lonnie.

"Hey!" Abigail calls out, still sailing.

Lonnie yells hey right back. "What are y'all doing here?" he asks.

"What's it look like, goofball?" Abigail says. "We're just hanging around."

"Us too." Lonnie grabs the third swing and gets to cranking. There's not a fourth swing to be had, so Sam hops up to catch a rung of the monkey bars. It's not much of a hop. Over Christmas break, he shot up about a foot, and now he's a long-legged kid. He dangles from the bar and does a few chin-ups.

Abigail says, "Watch out, Sam. Lu's a champion at monkey bars."

"I know," he says. "I remember." *He remembers!* Abigail acts like this is no big deal, so I keep my trap shut and swing higher and higher. *Creak whine, creak whine.* Does he like me?

Soon, Abigail jumps off her swing and offers it to Sam. She takes a couple of turns going down the slide, and Sam moseys over to the swing. Lonnie's cranking faster and higher, like me. All the while, Abigail's going *wheee* as she zips down the slide and runs around to the ladder for another scramble to the top. So long as they're making noise, I can just sail into the trees and not worry about talking to Sam, although I *am* thinking about him. A lot.

After a while, Sam yells up at Lonnie, "It's almost time for us to go."

"Aw, shoot!" Lonnie is practically in the treetops, and it takes him a while to slow his swing down. I bring my swing in for a landing, too.

"I bet y'all don't know where we're going Saturday," Abigail says. "To the international club."

"What international club?" Sam says, twirling the chain of his swing in a slow circle.

"Tell him, Lu."

"Well, there's this big dinner a couple of times a year at a college in Birmingham. Scads of people who moved here from other ountries go to it. There's even a talent show and a kids' area with games and stuff."

"Hey, that sounds really cool!" Sam says. "I wish I could go."

Abigail comes off the slide and stands near the swings, hands on hips. "You know what, Lu? You ought to invite Sam to go with us."

Sam's head jerks up. He puts a foot out to stop the twirling motion.

What is she *doing*? I throw her some signals, like a slice across the throat. But she pays me no mind. "Lu's whole family goes—and her neighbors, the Sampredos. This'll be my first time, and it's going to be great."

Abigail keeps giving me the eye, and I keep giving her the frown. She's waiting for me to invite him for real, but she must be off her rocker. Forget it. I'd die of embarrassment. Not to mention that Mamá would never let me invite a boy to anything—not till I'm pushing thirty and have a headful of gray hair. Plus, even in the Sampredos' dinosaur of a Cadillac, there isn't room for that many people. Grrrr, I'm going to strangle you, Abigail!

We all leave the playground, with Abigail and me going east, and Sam and his brother heading up an alley that cuts toward their house. When they're out of earshot, Abigail gets right to it. "Why didn't you invite him?"

"Are you crazy? You know my parents! I can't get permission to take a boy!"

"Why not? Boys aren't poison. And anyway, Sam's dad is a preacher."

"Right. Tell that to my mother."

"She married a boy, didn't she?"

"Jeez, I'm nowhere close to getting married!"

"But doesn't your sister go out on dates with boys?" Abigail asks.

"Barely. Nobody can get near her unless our parents approve. That's how they do it in Argentina."

"Eek! Tell them to get with the program already. This is America, land of the free."

"Humph, not in my house!"

We start pedaling up the street. And right there, in front of God and everybody, she yells, "Poor you! You're going to be an old maid!" Thanks a lot, Abigail.

We chug up the hill. Since Abigail's ready to melt, we get off our bikes and walk them for a bit. "So you'll call Phyllis?" I say.

"Yeah." *Huff, huff, huff.* "Or talk to her at school."

"Not at school! Missy won't let you!"

"Good point." We reach the corner of Greene and Early. "You better not tell your parents that boys are invited to that party or you won't get to go. Poor you!"

Golly, she's right about that. "See you tomorrow." And I take off pedaling, fast—much faster than Abigail—before she can yell any more "poor you"s.

★ 7 ★
VICTORY DANCE

Mrs. Underwood adjusts her mirrored sunglasses and stations herself at the chalk line, whistle at the ready. All day, I've been dreaming about running this driveway. I'm about to find out if I can make lightning strike twice or if yesterday's run was nothing more than a fluke.

As soon as she lets the whistle fly, good and shrill, we're off. Once again, most of the girls take off at full speed. Not me. Past the pothole, past the teachers' parking lot, and past the first curve, I keep a steady clip going and watch while girls drop away like dogwood petals in a storm. Opposite the band room, a girl veers off into the grass and leans over, hands to knees. Lord a mercy, she's saying goodbye to her lunch!

Missy and Phyllis have already slowed down to a Sunday stroll. This morning in homeroom, Phyllis slipped me a real invitation on the sly, like Missy isn't supposed to know. So I guess I *am* going to the party after all.

Soon, the rest of the class is a far piece back. It's down to Belinda, Angie, Connie, and me. When Connie sees me gaining, her eyes say, "Uh-oh." We go stride for stride past the flagpole. I can tell Connie wants to beat me in the worst way. Everything's long on Connie: her hair, her nose, her face, and, most important of all, her legs. So it's a heck of a surprise that I can outrun her, but that's what happens. Next, it's adios to Angie.

Now that I'm alongside Belinda, the time for holding back is done. Our legs and arms pump like gangbusters. She's breathing hard. I'm breathing hard. We push down the stretch to the last curve by the ball fields and back around toward the starting line. We're nearly at our limit when Mrs. Underwood sees us and starts hollering. My body stretches for the finish, and although I get there first, there's but a flea's eyelash between Belinda and me.

Mrs. Underwood goes off like a rocket on the Fourth of July. "Good golly, Miss Molly, God bless America, and the good Lord be praised! I got me some runners for next year!" She dances like ants have invaded her pants. Belinda and I bust out laughing.

On the far side of the chalk line, we pace back and forth, giving our lungs a chance to catch up. She says, "Girl, you are fast."

"So are you."

"Next time, I'm gonna get you." She grins at me.

I grin back. "Maybe, maybe not."

She keeps smiling. "Don't count your chickens."

"You neither." We're all smiley. It's like my mouth is stuck in a goofy grin and so is hers. I like her. I really do.

Angie strides in, heehawing about Mrs. Underwood and her shimmy.

"Come on, Lu, do a victory dance with us!" Belinda says.

I shake my head. "I'm no good at dancing."

"Don't worry about that," she says.

But that's not the real problem. What's really got me worried is crossing over a line I'm not supposed to cross, if people see me getting friendly with Belinda and Angie. I'm already on the outs as it is, being Loser Olivera and all. Seems like I can't be too careful.

Connie arrives and plunks herself on the curb, huffing for all she's worth. She doesn't look at us; instead, she runs the toe of her shoe along dandelions springing up from cracks in the cement. I don't dare speak to anybody with that sulky a face.

At long last, here comes the rest of the gang, dragging

their behinds across the finish. Some fire dirty looks our way. Abigail's hobbling. I help her back inside the locker room, where she peels her socks off, and wouldn't you know it: a blister the size of Texas.

★8★
DIPPITY-DO

Of all the things I could've gotten from Papá, why oh why did it have to be his hair and not something better, like one of umpteen things he's good at? At Ochs' Fine Jewels, where he works, he clips an eye loupe to his glasses and repairs busted-up watches, left and right. He engraves silver platters with the prettiest monograms you ever did see. He's also really good at singing and playing the guitar. Me, I'm fumble fingers and can't carry a tune except in my head. But look at my hair: I got his porcupine quills all right. Thanks a lot, Papá.

Tonight, I sit in front of the TV with a dripping head and a towel on my shoulders, sectioning my hair off with a rattail comb. Since it refuses to curl on its own, I have to slather each section with this setting gel called Dippity-do. Next, I roll up the Dippity-do'd strand in a foam curler. According to the package, foam is supposed to make the curlers comfy enough to sleep in, but that's a lie.

Normally I wouldn't go to all this trouble, but tomorrow's the international club. It's a big deal, and Marina and I are expected to dress like proper ladies. Mamá can't stand how lots of the older girls show up looking va-va-voom, their hair teased up into bouffants and their false eyelashes going flutter-flutter. Some of the younger girls are just as glamorous, parading around in loud dresses and high-heeled shoes.

Even if Mamá would allow it, I'm not so swift in the glamour department. In fact, Abigail thinks I need an education, so she dumped her old issues of *Groovy Gal* on me. They're full of beauty tips and advice on boys. Guess I ought to be studying those things like crazy, but I haven't gotten around to it yet.

The candidates are on TV tonight. When Governor Brewer comes on, explaining why everybody should vote for him, Papá soaks it up. "There's a true statesman. He makes Alabama look good." I think I know what Papá means. Alabama didn't look so hot when George Wallace had it last. Black people had to fight for every little bitty thing, like the right to eat in restaurants and sit wherever they pleased at the movies, and Wallace did everything he could to stop them. That's just plain wrong.

By the time Brewer finishes his spiel, my hair-rolling is done. I settle down on the couch, and our cat, Ringo, takes over my lap.

Just then, Wallace comes on, and Papá changes the channel lightning fast. "I'm not giving two seconds to that scoundrel. Let's see what else is on."

Fine by me—the news is a big snore anyway. The other channel is running the dumbest movie ever, *Tarzan in the Valley of Gold*, but the fake-looking stunts make Papá and me laugh.

When the movie finishes, Ringo is so cozy in my lap that I hate to budge. Next thing I know, I'm zooming around the school driveway. The crowd is on my side. *Lu, Lu! Lu—Lu—Lu!* With their feet going like thunder on the bleachers, it's no wonder that I'm flying to the finish line in record time. Then Mamá shakes me awake. "Go to bed, hija. Tomorrow's a big day."

ROAD ALPHABET

"You look pretty!" Abigail says as she slides into the back-seat next to me.

"So do you!" We're both in fancy dresses, and our hair is rolled and sprayed till it can't wobble or spring loose. International club, here we come!

With Papá behind the wheel of the Sampredos' Cadillac, we head north. Next to Papá in the front seat, Mamá and Mrs. Sampredo yakety-yak in Spanish. Mamá says it's a crying shame that Mr. Sampredo had to work tonight. Mrs. Sampredo says, "¡Sí, pues!"

The Sampredos are my parents' best friends. There are no other foreigners in Red Grove besides our family and theirs. We're the Argentines, and they're the Cubans. Papá says Spanish is the Elmer's glue that holds us together. Plus, we're catty-corner neighbors that borrow eggs and sugar back and forth. Mamá and Mrs. Sampredo drive up to Saint Stanislaus Catholic Church for mass nearly every weekend, and Papá and Mr. Sampredo get together to watch boxing matches on TV.

In the English-only corner of the backseat, Abigail says, "See what I brought?" She pulls a small book covered in red leatherette out of her purse.

"What's that for?"

"For addresses and phone numbers, in case I make new friends tonight."

Jeepers. Never crossed my mind to get anybody's address. I flip through the book and see entries for most of our white classmates. Under the *H*s, there's Phyllis Hartley, at 46 Pecan Orchard Drive, a house I know inside out.

I keep flipping through the book. *I, J, K, L, M . . .* There's a section labeled *Mc*, and Sam McCorkle's address is the only one in it: 306 Periwinkle, which is right behind his father's church. Of course, since it's a boy's house, I've seen it only from the outside.

The ride takes us through piney woods and teensy towns. I get the bright idea to start a game of road alphabet. Abigail nabs *A* off some billboard. I rack up a twofer with Berean Church (*B* and *C*). She picks up *D* for Dairy Fresh and tries to make a case for claiming the *F,* too, but I say no way. "*E* comes next, and you're not allowed to skip letters."

"Wait. You got two off Berean Church. That's against the rules."

"You're making that up!"

"Am not!" We're noisy as chickens. Marina is on the other side of me in the backseat, where she turns the pages of her French novel like we're not even alive.

"Your sister's such a brain," Abigail whispers.

"I know, but let's not tell her."

Election signs have sprouted all over the roadside, like ugly weeds. Lieutenant governor. State treasurer. Judge this, judge that. Perfect for road alphabet.

"*N* for Norris!" I yell out. "O'Brien—that's an O!"

Abigail shouts, "Pearson!"

Papá chuckles. "Girls, can you quiet down a little?"

We giggle and whisper our next few calls. Signs that say WALLACE are plastered all over, and we call for *W* at the same time.

Abigail yelps, "Do over!" Marina glances up from her book and shakes her head, which makes us giggle all the more.

★ 10 ★
THE RACE

"Welcome to the United Nations of Alabama!" Papá says, walking us through the door of the meeting hall. He's looking snappy in a coat and tie and shiny shoes. He holds his guitar case in one hand and props the doors open with the other. Inside, flags from the nations of the world hang from the ceiling, fluttering in the breeze from the air-conditioning. There's a stage with a microphone on a stand, and scads of tables and chairs lined up in front of it. Everywhere you look, boocoodles of people mill around, jabbering all at once in who knows how many languages. Mamá and Mrs. Sampredo get swallowed up in the crowd as they carry the dishes they made to the food tables. I hear a lady say, "Ooh, Claudia, are those your famous empanadas?" Empanadas are South American meat pastries that we always bring to the club.

Mamá answers, "¡Claro qué sí!"

I think Abigail's mouth might be stuck in the open position. "I never knew there were so many foreigners in Alabama!" When we finally make it to the buffet line, she scoops some tandoori chicken, Swedish meatballs, and pad thai onto her plate. "Aw, shoot! Your mom's empanadas are all gone!"

I spy Irina, a girl I usually hang around with at these meetings. She waves like mad. "Over here, Lu!" She's sitting with a bunch of other kids our age. Abigail wastes no time introducing herself, and before you know it, that little red address book is making the rounds.

We're finishing dinner when the microphone squeals to life. A man with a beard says, "May I have your attention, please?" He's the club president, Mr. Chandar. People hush talking and turn to face him. "Continue eating, if you wish, while we start the talent show."

First, a troupe of dancers from Thailand takes the stage. After that come singers, piano players, violinists, and a band of Greek musicians that gets us out of our seats dancing. I lock arms with Irina on one side and Abigail on the other, and we've got smiles plastered to our faces that won't quit.

After a bunch more acts, Mr. Chandar is back at the

microphone. "And now for a special treat. You know this performer very well. He and his lovely wife and daughters have been a part of this club for years. Please welcome our former club president, Francisco Olivera!"

When Papá pulls the microphone closer, my nerves go all a-tingle. He strums the opening chords, and a murmur starts up. It's "Guantanamera," a song everybody loves. His fingers pluck the guitar strings, and his shiny black shoes tap out the rhythm. The way the microphone sends his voice across that huge room—gosh, it makes my throat feel like a big ole egg's stuck in it.

Abigail grabs my arm. "You never told me he could sing like that!"

Irina whispers, "Luuuuu, he sounds like a record!"

All I can do is nod and wipe my eyes.

Afterward, the grown-ups drink coffee and yak about boring stuff. Soon the hallway leading out from the meeting room is crammed with kids escaping to our own world. I hurry alongside Irina. "Did you bring your Yahtzee game?"

"Yep. And Clue and dominoes and two decks of cards."

"Oh my gosh, this is the best fun I've had in ages!" Abigail squeals. She and a girl named Katya skip off down the hall together. Jeez Louise, how come *I'm* such a turtle at making friends?

We sixth-graders end up in Room 105. Somebody with

a portable record player finds an outlet to plug it into, and after that the records never stop spinning. Since Marina and I play music day and night, I can sing along with most any song you care to name. I'm sort of in love with Van Morrison right now, on account of his song "Brown Eyed Girl." It feels like he could be singing about *me*.

A group of us plop down on the floor for Yahtzee. I rattle the dice in the cup and throw a straight. When "Somebody to Love" by Jefferson Airplane comes on, one of the boys turns up the volume. It's a cool song, but not really my thing. By the time I roll the dice again, a new one has started: "Stand!" by Sly and the Family Stone. *Now* we're talking—this one is really far out, and lately, Spider's been playing the ever-living mess out of it.

Just when it feels like we're going to do nothing but play board games all night, somebody yells, "They're about to race!" and my ears go *boing*, like antennae tracking a signal. Seems like I'm thinking about racing all the time these days. I run to see what's going on, with Abigail and Irina right behind me.

Six boys are lined up out in the hall, which looks a mile long, with nothing but smooth, waxed floor between here and the wall of elevators at the very end. "On your marks, get set, *go*!" someone calls. The boys bolt out of there, arms and legs a-thrashing. Once they reach the wall, they spin

back around toward the finish line. It's all over in about fifteen seconds, and all of us watching go bananas screaming.

When the noise dies down, the kid in charge says, "Who
wants to go in the next round?"

I pop up like a jack-in-the-box. "Me!" Don't ask me how
I got the nerve to do that—it sort of happened before my
brain figured out where my mouth was headed.

Abigail's eyes get huge. "Are you bonkers?"

The kid in charge says, "Nope, boys only."

"How come? Why can't girls race?" I ask. But nobody pays
me any mind. I have to watch two more races before they
give in and let me run. Then I kind of wonder if I *am* bonkers, because it's me against three boys, all taller by bunches.
At the word *go*, we tear out. Well, the boys tear out. Their
sneakers make easy ground on the waxed linoleum, but my
patent-leather shoes can't get traction for love or money. I
come in last. *Dead* last. The girls rush over to me, saying I
was brave to try. But I don't feel brave; I feel cruddy.

Abigail clucks at me. "Lu, don't worry! You can't be
expected to win against boys! Come on, let's go play cards."

I shake my head. "I'm racing again."

"Lu! You'll only embarrass yourself."

"But I *have* to try again! Don't you get it?"

"Good grief, you're impossible."

Before the racers line up, I dash to the ladies' room,

where I kick off my shoes and peel off my pantyhose. Now, the way that my bare toes feel on the slick floor tells me it's going to be different this time. Sure enough, at the word *go*, I take off like a bandit.

The hall's a blur. White squares of linoleum whiz by under my bare feet, just like in my dreams. I touch the far wall, spin back around, and boogie for the finish, trailing the fastest boy by only a teensy bit. And in the end, I beat two boys. *Two boys!*

Cheers echo all over. Down the hall, doors fly open and younger kids pop their heads out to see what the dickens is going on. Guess I'm lost in a victory daze, because Abigail has to jerk on my sleeve to wake me up. "Your mother!" she hisses.

I whirl around, and there's Mamá, parked on a shiny square of white floor, her arms folded across her chest and her eyes aiming a dagger right at my bare feet. "Lu, put your shoes on right away. We're leaving. *Now*."

It's hot in the backseat and I'm begging for air. Abigail opens the window, but only a crack. "Your hair's gone wacko," she tells me. "Wind will only make it worse." What could be worse than what's already happened? It felt like a hundred pairs of eyes were on me when Mamá showed up.

Speaking of Mamá, she's still fuming. Mrs. Sampredo turns partway around to shoot me a look that says, *poor you*. It's Papá who opens his mouth. "Lu, I'm very surprised at you. You're much too old for playing such childish games in public—and in your beautiful dress, which your mother worked so hard to sew for you!"

My face stings like all get out. At least he says this in Spanish, although I'm sure Abigail has no trouble figuring out that he's scolding. She doesn't dare say a word. She just squints in the dark at her little red book. Me, I run my fingers through my hair, yanking out hardened globs of Dippity-do. Stupid hair.

After a while, Papá, Marina, and Mrs. Sampredo break the silence and get to talking about politics, halfway in English, halfway in Spanish. The more they gab, the better I feel, because it's lots better than icy quiet. Mrs. Sampredo has loads to say about the revolution in Cuba. Papá has loads to say about dictators in Argentina. And we already know about the bee in Marina's bonnet: she's dying to keep Wallace out of office.

Finally, Mamá stops fuming about my running long enough to speak up. "Please, hija," she says to Marina. "People don't like foreigners to meddle. Please don't try to fix America's problems!"

"I'm not trying to fix America's problems," says Marina. "Just Alabama's!"

Mamá says, "I won't have you going around making trouble."

"But, Mamá, if people don't stand up to oppressors, how else will justice—"

Papá jumps in. "Ladies, let's give it a rest for now, shall we? We're all on the same side, Marina. Your mother and I worry sometimes that you might stick your neck out too far."

"We're not like everyone else," Mamá warns. "If the white people in this town got mad at the McCorkles for protesting, just imagine how they would treat us!"

Abigail whispers to me, "What did she mean about the McCorkles?"

"You know he went to jail, right?"

"Sam's dad? Why?"

Sometimes I forget that Abigail didn't live in Red Grove, or even Alabama, when these things happened. I get Marina to explain. "Lots of protestors got arrested," she says, "but they didn't do anything to deserve it. See, the people in power were trying to stay in power, so they made things as hard as they could on anyone speaking out."

Abigail says, "Oh," and I get the feeling that for once in her life, the cat's got her tongue.

A few miles pass before I remember that Abigail didn't get any empanadas. "Mamá, the empanadas were all gone by the time Abigail went through the buffet line. "

Mamá says, "Don't worry, Abigail. I'll make some *just for you*. It might take me a while, though, because I have to finish this wedding dress first!" Every dollar she earns from this wedding will help her buy a plane ticket to visit our family in Argentina. She and Mrs. Sampredo gab about how long it's been since Mamá's last trip down there—more than five years.

And that's when I notice Papá's eyes in the rearview, smiling again. I flop back against the backseat and breathe easier.

Abigail whispers, "Don't forget about the cakewalk this Friday. We can go straight from my house, and if you come over early, you can help me bake the cake."

"Cool by me."

The miles zip by. Pretty soon, my mind drifts back to when my speed kicked in and the hall turned to a blur under my feet. Gosh, running fast is the best feeling in the world! It's sinking in: I want to prove Mrs. Underwood right on Field Day—that I *can* run like the blue blazes. Whatever the blue blazes is, that's how fast I want to be.

★12★
BOOM CHAKALAKAH

Homeroom is wild this Monday morning. Half the boys are drumming on their desks with pencils. *Boom boom boom chakalakah boom boom boom chakalakah*. But no matter the racket, Belinda's eyes stay glued to the pages of her book. Golly Moses, she's the first bookworm I've met who can hold a candle to Marina.

Right before the first bell, Abigail bursts in. "Yoo-hoo! I just went to the office and changed my schedule for next year."

"You did?" I say.

"Yep. Next time we go to the international club, I'm going to be ready, because I'm taking Spanish now!"

"Hey," Sam says, whirling toward her, "so am I."

"Cool beans!" Abigail answers. "How do you say it in Spanish, Lu? Beans *fritos*?"

I snort. "Not *fritos*—that means fried!"

"You should hear her talking with her mom and dad," Abigail says. "She can say anything in Spanish. Ask her." Sam eyeballs me to see if Abigail's telling the truth, but I'm keeping my trap shut. The truth is, my Spanish isn't so hot.

Still, now that I have Sam's attention, I'd like to hold on to it. His fountain pen is out and so is one of his spiral-bound notebooks, where he's always doodling on the back cover. He follows my gaze. "Sometimes I like to draw stuff, just for kicks." He smiles at me. Now my pulse goes *boom boom boom chakalakah*.

At eight on the dot, Mrs. Donnelly calls roll, leads us in the Pledge of Allegiance, and starts in on announcements, which usually bore us cross-eyed. But I hear a smile in her voice when she reads that Spider's been appointed to the math honor society. Pretty much everybody breaks into cheers, which end with Spider standing up to take a bow. Next, she calls out the names of kids who made it into the marching band: Chad, Sam, and Melody. We clap about that, too.

When Mrs. Donnelly gets to the part about a new dress code for next year, one that allows us girls to wear pants, every biddy in the room starts cheeping. "Don't get too excited," Mrs. Donnelly warns. "Only pantsuits will be allowed, not blue jeans."

Tons of girls go, "Awwww, shucks!" No skin off my nose; Mamá would never let me wear blue jeans to school even if the dress code allowed it.

Missy says, "Big woo, this doesn't even pertain to me."

Connie says, "Because you're going to East Lake?"

It's a perfectly innocent question, but Missy gives her a glare straight out of the deep freezer. "Why else?"

Mrs. Donnelly cuts in. "Everyone take out your composition folders."

All this time, I've been sneaking glances at Belinda, who must not give a horse's patootie about dress codes. She's too buried in the pages of that book.

★ 13 ★

THE CHALKBOARD

"What's taking so long?" I've got energy to burn and no way to burn it. But Mrs. Underwood's off in the distance, having a chitchat with the band director. While the cat's away, the mice are lazing under the tulip trees.

"Hush your mouth, Lu!" Abigail says. "The longer she beats around the bush, the better."

"Not for Lu," Paige says, poking me in the ribs. "She's teacher's pet."

"Am not."

"Oh, yes, you are, and you know it, you little stinker," Abigail says with a sly grin.

I grin back because it's kind of true, but I still can't

believe that Mrs. Underwood thinks *I'm* anything special. Mrs. Underwood!

Missy is over there telling everybody that her mother is in charge of the committee deciding on new school uniforms for East Lake. Connie gets bright-eyed and bushytailed when Missy announces that the skirts will be plaid and the blazers will have fancy crests on the pockets, just like prep schools up north. "I wish so bad I could go," we overhear Connie say.

Abigail rolls her eyes. "I wouldn't go there just for the *uniforms*," she tells me and Paige.

The band director yells, "One, two, three," and then the drums go to town. Finally, Mrs. Underwood steps up to the chalk line and lets out a bellow. "Visiting hours are over, ladies!" Over the groans, she barks at us to line up. The whistle goes off, and within seconds, the fastest girls charge their way to the front.

Belinda and I run side by side and keep a watch on the leaders, but when we reach the marching band, swirling flags block our view for a stretch. Half the marchers take a hard turn, bringing the brass section to the edge of the driveway. Trombones blare in my ear. And here come the tuba players, swinging their big ole horns left and right, in time to the music. That's when I catch a flash of Sam—or at least the side of his face—on the shiny brass curves of his marching tuba. I stare longer than I should, and it slows me down a step. Jeepers, I hope I'm not going boy crazy!

At the flagpole, Belinda and I haul it. Before long, we pass Angie, but Connie, she's a fireball on legs today. Our sneakers spit gravel as we zoom around the last bend, gaining on her, inch by inch. She knows it, too; every so often, she checks over her shoulder to see where we are. Mrs. Underwood's at the chalk line, hollering and clapping. "Come on, girl! It's your turn to shine!" *Whoosh*. Connie sweeps across the finish before we can catch her, and Mrs. Underwood does a jig.

In the locker room, Connie glows like somebody found her plug and stuck it in a socket. Can't blame her. I'd be tickled pink, too. Guess word travels fast, because in social studies, Chad and Nick greet her with a goofy chorus of "My Bonnie Lies over the Ocean," except they sing *Connie* in place of *Bonnie*. She blushes like nobody's business.

Miss Garrett stands over Nick and Chad. "All right, enough of that!" Then she claps her hands to get the attention of the whole class. "Get settled in, everyone. It's time for your homework check." Just as I'm pulling my election notebook out of my book bag, I hear Miss Garrett snap, "Who wrote this?" Kids start snickering, and I whirl around. On the chalkboard, I read the words "Loser Olivera" right before Miss Garrett's eraser wipes them clean.

I know darn well who wrote it: Missy. Or Phyllis. Why do they have to be so mean?

Sam nudges me. "That was dumb. Just ignore it."

I shrug like it's nothing. The bell pierces through all the chatter, and that's when Missy and Phyllis sashay through the door with their hair freshly fluffed and tied back with ribbons.

Oh. So it *wasn't* Missy who wrote it? Great, now some other meanie is on my case.

At the bus loading zone, Belinda says, "We're not letting Connie have it that easy again, are we?" She's in a bouncy mood, and I wish I could feel the same, but I'm stuck on what I saw on the chalkboard. "Girl, you better not be moping about a silly ole race!"

"I'm not!" I manage a teensy smile.

The doors of Belinda's bus pop open, and kids hurry up the steps. "Toodle-oo till tomorrow, Peewee!" she says, waving her fingers at me. Peewee. She called me Peewee. I smile, and this time, it feels real.

★ 14 ★
MARINA

"Lu, come on. It was just a joke," says Abigail.

"But who did it?" I have to remember to keep my voice down on the phone because Mamá's in the dining room on the sewing machine and she'll pester me with a million questions.

"Beats me," Abigail says. "It happened before I got to class."

I pace back and forth, as far as the phone cord will let me. "Missy wasn't there, but I bet you anything she made somebody else do it."

"Well, *I* wouldn't know!"

"Don't you dare cover for Missy!"

"Why would I cover for *her*?"

"Because you're scared of her?" I say.

"Hush your mouth! You're more scared of her than I am!"

"She's getting worse—that's why!"

Abigail doesn't argue with that. "Just play it cool for a while and she'll forget about you."

"Play it cool how?"

"You know—don't show off or anything."

A ball of confused feelings churns inside my gut. Abigail's good at lots of things, like making friends and stuff. Missy's good at fashion and hairdos. Can't *I* be good at something, too—like running?

"Calm down," Abigail says. "Missy's going to East Lake next year, remember? So everything will go back like it used to be."

"I know. Sorry to be such a worrywart."

"Take two aspirin and call me in the morning," Abigail says, and I can tell she's grinning like an imp, which is one of my favorite things about her.

The kitchen table is covered with posters that Marina is making for Governor Brewer's campaign. Her blue marker squeaks around the loop of the *B* in Brewer. While I watch her, I chugalug a glass of orange juice. "Guess what, Marina?"

"What?" She pushes her hair back from her face and starts on the *R*.

"I might be getting a new friend. And she's got brains, so you can stop pestering me about that."

"That's cool! Who is it?"

"You don't know her. Belinda Gresham."

She looks up from the poster. "Maybe I do, or at least, I might know her parents. Is her dad Dr. Gresham?"

"*Doctor* Gresham? She never said anything like that." Come to think of it, Belinda and I haven't talked about anything except running and crazy ole Mrs. Underwood. I keep meaning to ask her about that book she's always got in front of her face, but I haven't done it yet.

"You could check in the phone book under *Gresham*," Marina says.

"Good idea." I grab the phone book and rustle the pages to the Gs. There's just one listing for a family named Gresham, which means her dad *must* be Dr. Gresham. "It says they live on Beaumont Street. Where's that?"

"Over on the west side of town."

"Never been there." I guess that's where lots of black people live.

Ringo shows up and starts rubbing against Marina's leg. "Well, if she's your friend, you ought to visit her sometime. And bring her over here to see us."

"Maybe." That gets me to thinking about Belinda's house. I bet her bedroom has bookshelves up the wazoo, crammed with paperbacks. I wonder what she'd think of my bedroom, with weird things like yellow newspaper clippings stuck to a corkboard. "You know why I'm getting friendly with Belinda? We're both pretty good runners. Mrs. Underwood's getting us ready for Field Day."

"She's a runner, too?" Marina asks. "I knew you were good. I was at the international club, remember?"

I clamp my hands over my ears. "Don't remind me of that night."

"Why not?" She caps her marker and stops to pour food into Ringo's bowl. "You raced against boys! That had me busting my buttons."

"It *did*? Not Mamá and Papá—they were spitting mad."

"Aw, heck. Mamá's old-fashioned. She doesn't even think girls belong in sports. Get used to it, Lu, or it'll drive you bananas."

"But what about Papá? He loves sports."

"True, but he loves Mamá even more."

I let out a long, ragged sigh. Mamá and Papá have been in this country plenty long by now, long enough to get with the program. This is supposed to be the land of the free, or haven't they heard?

★ 15 ★
GRAPE NEHI

Like a good little sister, I pick up the posters Marina made yesterday and head downtown to drop them off at Brewer's local campaign headquarters. It's a short walk, especially for a speed demon like me, itching to get back to air-conditioning on this scorching-hot day. Abigail has promised to meet me there.

At headquarters, stacks of mail are everywhere. Boxes of bumper stickers peep out from under tables. Mimeograph machines rattle. Coffeepots gurgle. On the walls, there are giant posters of Governor Brewer in his elegant best, smiling over the words FULL TIME FOR ALABAMA. It seems like his eyes follow me as I cross the room, so I move faster.

Toward the back of the room, I spy Marina. She's got a

phone pressed to one ear and a finger stuck in the other, on account of so many volunteers gabbing on phones nearby.

I plunk the posters down on a stack of boxes. Marina nods at me, all the while talking to somebody about voting in next Tuesday's primary election. As soon as she gets off the phone, she says, "Thanks, Lu. You saved me a trip to the house. Want a doughnut or some lemonade? They're in the break room."

"Not now. Abigail's coming by in a minute." But when lots of minutes go by and Abigail doesn't show up, Marina puts me to work sweeping up paper. Later, the door opens and here comes Sam's father, with Lonnie in tow. I look for Sam, but he's not with them.

Lonnie makes a beeline to where I'm sitting. "What are *you* doing here?"

"Not much. What are *you* doing here?"

"Nothing."

"Where's your brother?"

"He's out there helping that friend of yours with her bike."

"He is?" I stow the broom and head outside.

Sure enough, on the sidewalk not too far up the block, Abigail is holding her bicycle steady while Sam crouches next to it, checking one of the tires. "I know how to pump it," he says. "Let's walk over to Handy's and I'll do it for you."

Abigail sees me coming. "Sorry I'm late, but this stupid bike keeps giving me fits."

Sam unfolds his lanky self. "Hi, Lu." A little something stirs inside me, kind of like a fish in a bucket doing flip-flops.

The three of us walk down to Handy's, a gas station with a convenience store. It's only a few blocks away, but Sam insists on rolling Abigail's bicycle for her. The way his fingers clamp around the handlebars reminds me of how he holds his tuba. Wish I could work up the nerve to ask how it's going in the marching band. But with Abigail chattering nonstop, it doesn't matter if anybody else talks. She has two hundred things to say about the yearbook stuff she's working on, two hundred things I've already heard. But Sam doesn't look the least bit bored.

At Handy's, he pulls the air hose out of its stand and—*pfffft*—pumps up Abigail's tire, pretty as you please, like it's his everyday routine. His hands get smeared black from the tire, which Abigail makes a big fuss about.

"Don't worry. I can wash up later." He wipes sweat off his forehead, and now he's got a black smudge over one eyebrow.

Abigail digs into her pockets and pulls out some coins. "At least let me buy you a soda." She rushes inside Handy's and leaves me and Sam out in the heat. He props the bike up on its kickstand and leans over to squeeze the tire again. He keeps poking this and that all over her bike in case anything else is on the verge of giving out.

A thought washes over me. Maybe he likes *her*. Maybe *that's* why he got excited about the international club — to be with her.

Abigail hurries back with an orange Fanta and a grape Nehi. "You pick," she tells Sam.

"Gosh, you didn't have to," he mutters, taking the frosty bottle of grape soda out of her hand. He chugs it so hard that his Adam's apple bobs.

Abigail offers to split the Fanta with me, but I don't want any, even though it's hotter than a firecracker out here. It's just that I'm remembering how eager Sam got yesterday when she announced she was taking Spanish. He just about killed himself agreeing with her on everything. Suddenly, it's clear as day. *Of course* he likes her. Who wouldn't? She carries that little red address book all over creation because she wants to keep in touch with people, and she always knows what to say. Always. Plus, she's got those big blue eyes and that nice, soft hair that never needs Dippity-do.

Every smidgen of hope I had for Sam liking me is going down the tubes in a hurry. *Gurgle, gurgle, gurgle.*

"There's doughnuts in the break room at the head-quarters if y'all want some," Sam says.

"You must spend lots of time over there," Abigail says.

"Kind of. My parents are always volunteering."

We start walking back, but Sam tells Abigail she ought to test the tire, so she sets off pedaling up the block. She weaves back and forth from one lane to the other, yip-yipping like a coyote. Sam looks at me and grins. It's the first time I remember seeing his teeth. Gosh, nice teeth. Also, very nice eyes. Also, wavy brown hair that curls around his ears a tad. Even in this heat, I feel a blush coming on. But right behind it comes a wave of lonesomeness when I remember that he probably likes Abigail, not me. The fish in my gut does one more flip and then lies there, cold.

When we get back to the campaign offices, Sam leads us straight to the break room. His mother is in there, stir-ring a tall pitcher of lemonade. "Hi, kids!" She has the most cheerful face you ever saw, loaded with freckles, just like Lonnie's. She takes a gander at Sam tearing into the dough-nut box. "Whoa, there, kiddo. Didn't you eat lunch?"

"I better get back home," I tell Sam and Abigail, "or my mom will be worried."

Abigail says she'll walk with me as far as my house. Her newly pumped tire rolls over the sidewalk cracks and up to the first curb. When the light turns, we hurry across Shelby and then Cornelius.

"Guess what?" Abigail says. "I ordered me a set of detachable braids!"

"What for?"

"To look good, silly. Have you seen them in *Groovy Gal*, in those Nordic Gold ads? Four pairs only cost one dollar and ninety-five cents, plus four box tops. And that includes shipping and handling."

"You bought *four boxes* of Nordic Gold?"

"I had to! It'll take at least four braids for a hairdo! Plus, I've got to bleach my hair to match the braids, don't I?" Abigail's hair is light brown, so she's already more than halfway to blond. Me? Not even forty boxes of Nordic Gold could turn my dark hair blond.

"I just hope they get here in time for Phyllis's party," she adds.

"Why?"

"Lu, don't you care about looking good at the *party*? Boys are going to be there, for heaven's sake!"

"So? They see us at school every single day, looking like our regular selves."

"This is different. This is a *boy-girl party*—romances happen there. Don't you know anything?"

I think about that stack of *Groovy Gal* magazines under my bed. They're full of advice about crushes and parties and how to get boys' attention. Abigail has read every word of every page—and it shows.

No wonder Sam likes her.

★ 16 ★
HIGGLEDY-PIGGLEDY

Good news. Nobody has called me a loser since Monday.
For one thing, I've managed to beat the pack three days in
a row, even with Belinda nipping at my heels and Connie's
ponytail lashing me every time I pass her.

That Belinda's a crafty one. She's got a new trick—
making me laugh in the middle of a run. She does this by
shouting out goofy rhymes. It's got something to do with
that paperback she's reading, *The Book of Three*, which
I finally saw up close. There's a picture of a knight and a
horse and a pig on the cover. Weird. It's a sword-fighting,
magic-spell kind of book, the kind that boys usually go
for. And somebody in the story is always rhyming, which
Belinda seems to like—a *lot*. So say we're charging around

the last bend, making for the chalk line. She's liable to blurt out, "Higgledy-piggledy!"—knowing full well it'll crack me up. If I shake a fist at her, she'll add, "Shaking and quaking!"

Today, Belinda doesn't even need rhyming. She pulls ahead of me at the last curve, zooms down the stretch, and across the chalk line before I can catch her. "Ratsy patsy!" I yell after her, but she just laughs at me. Afterward, we flop down under the tulip trees. I tell her she should be a poet, and she says she already *is* a poet. She even has a notebook for her poems.

"Really?"

"Yep. I'll let you see it when you come to my house."

"Oh!" I'm so surprised that I don't know what to say next. I pull on a sprig of clover. The idea of going to her house flits around me like a butterfly with pretty wings. "Oh," I say again, like a dumb bunny, thinking about her notebook and her house—is it brick or wood? Is her dad a doctor-doctor or a college doctor?

"Hey, goofy, is 'oh' the only word you know?" she says. "It's just a house—nothing to be afraid of! The bogeyman doesn't live there." I fall back on the grass, laughing. Pretty soon, Angie joins us.

Connie doesn't show up for the longest time. She started off like a jackrabbit and ran out of gas before the flagpole. At long last, I spot her cutting across the lawn, heading straight for the locker room. Something's going kaflooey with her. Maybe she's sick, or maybe she's plumb had it with running.

While Mrs. Underwood huffs and puffs that the rest of the class is moving at the speed of molasses, the three of us find clover blossoms and start making a chain.

In the locker room, Belinda grabs a pen and writes my phone number on her hand. I write her phone number on mine. I *want* her number, but the whole time we're doing this, I'm jittery as a cat near water. If Phyllis or Missy catch me, it could start up another round of trouble—which Lord knows, I don't need. But I sure do want Belinda's number.

★ 17 ★
THE CAKEWALK

"Is this thing even working?" Abigail hollers into the hot oven. The cake is taking its sweet time. You're supposed to stick a toothpick in the middle to make sure it's all the way done. Trouble is, the toothpick keeps coming up gooey. After letting it go another five minutes, we yank both layers out of the oven, done or not.

It's already twenty minutes past six, and Mr. Farrow is driving us to the rally at 6:45 for the cakewalk. Good thing the icing is mixed and ready. Abigail takes a metal spatula and dives right in. I follow her lead with a spoon. We slather white icing between, around, and on top of the layers. She smooths, and I swirl, and when we finish, Abigail near about cries with happiness. "It's gorgeous," she breathes.

It *is* gorgeous—like a field of snow in one of those Christmas cards you always see.

We dash upstairs to clean up, and by the time we return to the kitchen—*boom*—the snow has melted. Globs of icing are on the move, slipping down the sides, leaving naked parts of cake showing.

Abigail screams, and Mr. Farrow hurries in to see what's the matter. When he catches sight of the cake, he slaps his forehead. "Silly girl, you have to let the cake cool down before you ice it."

"Now you tell me!" Abigail moans. "This is a disaster!" She and I run around in a panic, searching for edible stuff to hold down the icing: shredded coconut, gumdrops, chopped pecans, raisins. We stick everything, willy-nilly, all over that cake, and boy oh boy, does it ever look stupid when we're done. Bits of icing hang on for dear life to the gumdrops, and now the whole cake sags in the middle like a sorry old mattress.

Mr. Farrow tries hard not to laugh. Me, I don't say a word—Abigail's already in a stew. It takes two of us to lower the cake into the cardboard bakery box. While Abigail gets in the car, I hold the box and hand it to her oh so gently, like a newborn baby going home from the hospital in its mama's arms. An ugly baby.

★   ★   ★

You can see the fairground's field lights blocks away. Parked cars are backed up on both sides of the two-lane highway, so we have to walk a far piece along the grassy edge. The sound of a country-and-western band comes in loud and clear while we jostle elbow to elbow with people. "Watch it, I've got a cake in here," Abigail snaps.

Near the gate, Phyllis's brother, Jimbo, pops up out of the crowd. Back when I used to go to Phyllis's house a lot, Jimbo was actually nice to me. Most older brothers aren't like that. "There's my buddy Lu!" he says now. "What're you doing here? I figured y'all for Brewer people."

"We are, but—"

Abigail breaks in. "We're actually here for the cakewalk. It's the best fun!"

"Oh, yeah?" Jimbo says. "Speaking of fun, why don't you come over and play air hockey sometime?"

Dang, I'd forgotten all about the Hartleys' air-hockey table, but now that he brings it up, I sure have got a hankering to play. Too bad Phyllis and I aren't buddy-buddy these days.

Once he's gone, Abigail says, "You played air hockey with Jimbo Hartley? Isn't he a *junior*?" I can tell she's impressed, and that doesn't happen too often.

"I used to, way back when."

The jostling gets worse when we squeeze through the

gates. "Stay together, girls," Mr. Farrow says. He takes the cake box from Abigail and holds it over his head as we plow through the crowd.

The band we've been hearing ever since we turned the street corner is on the stage. All around are red and blue decorations and WALLACE FOR GOVERNOR signs. Rows of metal chairs face the stage, and people stream up and down, claiming seats by throwing purses and jackets over them. Grown-ups gather in clumps, shooting the breeze. Some line up to buy colas and snack foods at the concession stand. Seems like I know half the folks here, starting with our neighbors, the Mandersons. Over there are Mr. Abrams and his whole family. Now I see the postmaster and the ticket lady from the Velvet Cinema.

We make our way to the area marked out for the cake-walk. First, you've got to buy your ticket. PROCEEDS GO TO THE LOCAL WALLACE CAMPAIGN, a sign says—and that stops me in my tracks. "To the campaign?"

Abigail puts a hand on her hip. "What did you expect, goofy? This *is* a Wallace rally."

"I know, I know." But I'd almost forgotten about the *Wallace* part of it till now. Jeepers creepers, good thing I didn't tell Marina we were coming to the cakewalk. She would have my hide if she knew I'd gone anywhere near him or plunked down change for his campaign. Oh well, it's only fifty cents—surely Wallace can't perform any miracles with *that*.

Abigail heads straight for the cake display. The lady keeping watch over the donated cakes takes the box out of her hands and over to the crowded table.

"That's a whopping lot of cakes you've got there," Mr. Farrow says to the lady. "Are you sure you need my daughter's?" He throws Abigail a wink.

"I suppose you want to hog it for yourself," the lady says, grinning.

"Not specially." He laughs, and Abigail punches him on the arm.

A tall light pole casts its bright, bluish light on a corner of the field. Under it, in a flat grassy area, they've laid out a circle for the cakewalk. It's made of cardboard pieces with numbers stamped on them, set out like flagstones in a garden walkway. I take my stand on number twelve. Chad is right in front of me, and Robbie is ahead of him. They're already cutting up like the dickens, braying like donkeys and doing the funky-chicken dance. The man minding the record player for the cakewalk is giving them the evil eye.

Pretty much the whole white side of the sixth grade is already here, waiting for the start of the game. Not Sam, of course, and not Melody, who never goes anywhere outside of school except to clarinet lessons. But even Paige Donnelly is here, and I'm pretty sure her family doesn't care for Wallace's kind of politics. I guess she likes cakewalks, too.

"*Pssst*, Paige," I call to her. She wheels around to see who's talking.

"If your number's called, don't pick the cake in the red-and-white box."

"Why not?"

"Trust me. Just don't."

"Now you've got my curiosity up!"

Two more people show up, and now every number in the circle is taken. The man at the record player announces: "Ladies and gents, without further ado . . ." He sets the needle down and up starts the music. A fellow with a voice deeper than God's sings out: *"There was an old man named Michael Finnegan. He grew whiskers on his chin again."* It's a song we learned in first grade. Most of us walk along calmly like civilized human beings, but Chad and Robbie bunny-hop from one flagstone to the next, and now they're singing, too. *"The wind blew them off, and they grew in again. Poor old Michael Finnegan—begin again!"* Other boys join in, trying their best to sound like the booming voice on the record, which makes us girls giggle. Even Missy, across the circle from me, doubles over laughing.

The man lifts the needle off the record, and when the music stops dead, so do all the cakewalkers. You look down at your feet to see which number you're standing on. I'm on eight. The cake lady pulls a numbered golf ball out of a big jar and calls out, "Number seventeen! Number seventeen!" A high-school girl squeals and rushes over to claim herself a cake.

The music starts up again. It's the same singer, but a different song. Eight, nine, ten . . . I continue along the path of cardboard numbers. The boys won't stop cutting up, no matter how much the man at the record player harrumphs at them. I'm tickled sideways because it's always more fun when they put on a show.

"Number four! Number four!" That's Chad's number, but he wants to stay in the game, so they draw a second number. At this rate, we could be here all night—which I wouldn't mind, because I'm having a merry ole time. But three rounds later, the cake lady calls out: "Sorry, but the main program is about to start. I'm afraid we'll have to get back to the cakewalk afterward."

Everybody goes, "Awww, dang it!"

Mr. Farrow leads the way to rows of cars parked inside the fairground. People are using the cars as extra seating. We hop up on the hood of somebody's pickup truck and dangle our feet off the sides. It's like being at the drive-in movie on a summer night. Sitting up high, we can keep an eye out for our friends.

I'm smiling because it's so nice that they feel like my friends again. I haven't forgotten that somebody in my class wrote "Loser" on the chalkboard, but I figure it was just one the boys clowning around, since boys seem to love doing that. Well, not Sam. The Sam I used to know mostly kept his head down, fiddling with that fountain pen or cleaning his glasses. But the new Sam . . . well, I did catch him in a toothy grin the other day. The new Sam . . . uh-oh, that fish inside me starts going flip-flop—but now it's flip-flopping slower, like it's running out of air.

COME HEAR
GOV. WALLACE
at the
FAIRGROUNDS
TONIGHT!

★ 18 ★
THE RALLY

The program starts, and is it ever boring. A lineup of big-wigs sits on the stage, and each one takes a turn at the microphone, carrying on about how great Wallace is. After a while, people in the bleachers start chanting, "We want Wallace! We want Wallace!" Soon, more folks pick up the chant, and before you know it, pretty much the whole fair-ground is yelling it. Fine with me—the sooner he talks, the sooner we can get back to the cakewalk.

A man in a dark business suit bounces up the steps of the stage and works down the line of bigwigs, pumping hands. When the crowd realizes this is Wallace, they erupt into applause and whistles. The band cranks up again, this time with "Dixie." People jump to their feet, belting out the verses: "*In Dixie land where I was born early on a frosty morn, look away, look away, look away, Dixie land . . .*" Six huge Confederate flags wave above the crowd, and many little ones flutter like hummingbird wings in people's hands.

Wallace starts in on his speech. His voice booms through the speakers, saying stuff like, "They have taken away our control of public schools, and I aim to get it back." Wild cheering. "As soon as we get Sissy Britches out of the way, we can get back to running Alabama like it ought to be run." Wilder cheering.

I turn to Abigail. "What in thunderation is 'sissy britches'?" I have to shout, or she won't hear me.

Abigail asks her father, then yells his answer in my ear. "Wallace's nickname for Brewer!"

Sissy Britches? Calling our governor a name like that? Ugh. That is pure *mean*.

Wallace keeps going. He promises he's going to fix everything that Sissy Britches hasn't been man enough to fix. "School integration has been forced down our throats. The good white people of Alabama didn't ask for this!" The audience applauds like crazy.

I'm getting queasy. If he heard this kind of talk on TV, Papá would jump out of his chair to switch it off. And Marina? She'd sprout fangs that glow in the dark. But this crowd loves it.

Confederate flags dance like the devil everywhere you look. I get to thinking about Belinda and all the other black kids in my grade. It seems like everybody here would like nothing better than to boot them out of Red Grove Elementary and send them back to their old school. The queasy feeling climbs up into my throat and stays there. That's when a new thought comes to me: I don't belong here.

Thank goodness Wallace is just about done. "With your help, I'll put Alabama back on the right road. Can I count on your support?" The crowd roars, "*Yes!*"

"Dixie" starts up again, and you never heard such a racket. People are back on their feet, stomping, cheering, and whis-tling. I bet the graveyard's jumping. I bet the statues of Confederate soldiers on the courthouse lawn are saluting. I press my fingers to my ears but can't drown out the noise. *Wallace, Wallace, Wallace, Wallace!*

Now that it's over, several men move through the crowd, handing out flyers. Others do the same among the parked cars. We hop off the pickup's hood. When Abigail starts edging toward the cakewalk, Mr. Farrow says, "No, we're going home."

"Why, Daddy?" Abigail pleads. "We didn't finish the cake-walk!" But he cuts her off with a hard *no*. The two of us trudge behind him, making our way to the car. "He's awfully grumpy about something," Abigail mutters.

"Maybe he didn't like what Wallace said."

"Guess not." Abigail sounds real glum.

A group of girls skips past us, reciting in singsong voices: "Brewer is a sissy britches! Brewer is a sissy britches!" I look at Abigail to see her reaction. Her eyes are far off, and her mouth is in a pout. So I just trudge. And stew. And feel stupid for thinking this would be fun — even if it *started off* fun, which it did.

As we pass parked cars, I notice flyers under each set of windshield wipers. Mr. Farrow's Lincoln Continental has some on it, too. He yanks them off, and once we're in the car, he keeps the dome light on for a minute to look them over. His lips make a tight line. "Disgusting," he says, and balls up the flyers.

"Let me see them, Daddy!"

"No, Abigail. They're ugly and full of lies. You don't need to poison your mind with such things." He cranks the motor and steers out into the bumper-to-bumper traffic. Car horns blare left and right. People hoot and yell.

Abigail squeezes my arm and whispers, "Must've been really bad."

We stay quiet the whole ride back to the Farrows' house.

The farther we get from the noise and bright lights, the weirder everything gets in my mind. One minute we're at a cakewalk, having a blast, giggling at Chad and Robbie. The next minute, we're hearing all that mean stuff.

As we pull into the driveway, Mr. Farrow breaks the silence. "Girls, politics is a dirty game everywhere, but this is the worst I've ever seen. I feel pretty bad about taking you."

"But, Daddy, we didn't know it would be like that!"

"You didn't know, but *I* should have. I let you talk me into it, Abby, and that wasn't wise."

"But the cakewalk . . ."

"Oh, that blasted cakewalk." Mr. Farrow slams the car door. "You girls fend for yourselves, all right? I've got work to do in my office."

Abigail gets the cookie jar out. It's chock-full of snickerdoodles she made last night. They turned out lots better than the cake. She slaps a Paul Revere and the Raiders album on the stereo. After a while, the glum feelings start shrinking away into the shadows. We sing along with the record. We dance. We drool at the album photos of the lead singer, Mark Lindsay. By the time we've played the song "Kicks" three times in a row, the rally has started fading away and I feel pretty good.

★ 19 ★
BELINDA

If I had my druthers, I'd wipe last night's rally clean from my mind, like it never happened. Seems like Abigail's already done that. While she and her dad drive me home in the morning, she begs and begs to go see a movie called *The Computer Wore Tennis Shoes*, starring Kurt Russell. And if I know Abigail, Kurt's poster is going to be hanging on her bedroom wall pretty soon.

Mamá left today's newspaper neatly folded on my bed. She knows I need it for my election notebook. On the front page, there's a big article about the rally. After cutting it out and gluing it in my notebook, I figure that now I can forget I ever went.

Still, Madeline Manning stares at me from her photo on

my corkboard, and it feels like I owe her and all the black folks I know an explanation. "I didn't know it was going to be like that. I just wanted to go to the cakewalk, and I couldn't say no to Abigail. She's my best friend, see?"

But probably Madeline Manning wouldn't understand my sorry excuses, even if she could actually hear them. For one thing, she has tons of friends. They crowd the stadium seats, hollering their heads off while she holds up her brand-new gold medal and smiles for the cameras. I would be smiling, too. My mouth would get worn out from so much smiling.

I'm finishing my Saturday chores when the phone rings. "Three guesses who this is," a girl's voice says.

A happy feeling jumps on me. "Belinda?"

"Dang it, you're good!"

"What are you doing? Still reading that book?"

"Not anymore. I stayed up past midnight finishing it."

"I spent the night at Abigail's, and we stayed up late, too." As soon as those words pop out of my mouth, I'm wishing I could pop them back in. Lord knows I don't want to fess up to *Belinda* that I went anywhere near Wallace—no siree. That's when it comes to me how bad I want her for a friend. I really do.

"Don't you want to know why I'm calling?" she says.

"Sure."

"Let's go running, you and me."

"On a Saturday? What for?"

"So we can get ready for Field Day. Don't you want to get good enough to win?"

"Of course I do!"

We meet at the playground and tuck our bikes behind a clump of azaleas. Then, after a warm-up at our usual pace, we charge up the street like we mean business. There aren't many cars in this neighborhood, and the streets are shady. Granddaddy oaks curve over us with their arms full of springtime leaves. As we cruise along, I picture every part of the school driveway. This stop sign is right about where we'd see the pothole. This dip in the road is close to where we'd run through the patch of crabgrass. That garden behind a rickety wooden gate is just about even with the typing class. But I wonder just where on this street we'd round the last curve and see Mrs. Underwood with her feet spread wide, ready to break into a jig.

There's one thing this run has that our school driveway doesn't—a mean hill to climb. And boy, do my lungs notice. And boy, do my legs feel it. When we reach the top of the hill, Belinda is gulping for air, too.

"Ouch! That was hard!" I say between huffs.

"I second that," Belinda says.

Even though my legs feel like wobbly toothpicks, I'm not

one bit sorry we did this. Besides having ourselves a good run, it sure is a pretty day. The sky is clear, the shade is sweet, and twinkles of sunlight splash around us. Gosh, I feel the happiest I've felt in eons.

When we get back to the playground, Belinda says, "Let's go down the slide," which we do—a jillion times. We bust a gut laughing when the hem of my shorts gets hung on the ladder and she has to rescue me. It turns out that Belinda's a whiz at monkey bars, too. Her hands switch lightning-quick from bar to bar, and she goes *swoop*, upside down, before you can figure out how did she did it. I take a turn next, and don't you worry, I've got some tricks of my own.

★20★
RAINED OUT

Lightning goes *crack*, and the windows of the gym rattle. Rain pelts against the glass. On the other side of the canvas curtain that divides the gym in two, basketballs pound the wooden floor and sneakers thunder back and forth. Sounds like the boys are making a hailstorm over there. Man, that makes me jealous. I'd a lot rather be doing basketball drills instead of this—eleventy million sit-ups.

Mrs. Underwood barks out the rhythm. "Fifty-one, suck your gut in, fifty-two, get the lead out, fifty-three, all the way up . . ." By the time she gets to fifty-seven, she's glaring down at a girl who's starting to snivel. That girl better control herself, or we're liable to be here for another fifty. "Sixty-five, don't be lazy, sixty-six, keep it going . . ."

Suddenly, from the other side of the curtain, I hear Nick screech, "Quit hogging the ball, you turkey!"

And now Charles answers, "Get your nasty hands off me!" A tingle rockets up my spine. If there's one thing that scares me, it's when white boys and black boys start tussling with each other. I'm so afraid that everything will go upside down—the school, my friends, and even Red Grove. Golly bum, I guess I'm as bad a worrywart as Mamá.

I hear, "Try and make me!" It's Nick again.

Then Spider says, "Whoa, fellas! Take it eeeasy!" Hearing him on the other side of the curtain is just like hearing him on the radio announcing a song: "Here's the one and only Steeeeevie Wonder!" The whistle sounds for a new drill, and once again, the basketball pounds the floor in a steady drumbeat. Shoes squeak. A ball goes swish through the net, and a cheer goes up.

I wonder if anybody else noticed the boys' commotion. Not Paige. She's laid out like a fly under a flyswatter. Not Abigail, who's holding her stomach and looking woozy. Belinda is fixing her ponytail and showing no sign of worry. Didn't she hear them? But I think Belinda's friend Willa might've. She's up on her elbows, facing the gym curtains with a frown.

Then Mrs. Underwood bellows, "Now for push-ups!" and everybody groans.

In social studies, I watch for signs of anything brewing between the boys, but Charles doesn't raise a fuss and Nick minds his own beeswax. Miss Garrett reminds us that tomorrow is the day we've been waiting for — the primary election — and that we're expected to watch the returns. "If you don't have a television at home, be sure to make arrangements. You'll have a quiz on it Wednesday morning."

The bell rings, and we start to collect our things. When Sam pulls a stack of books out of his cubbyhole, I spot *The Book of Three* sitting on top, pretty as you please. My eyes bug out. "Hey, where did you get that book?"

"From Belinda. We swap books sometimes."

"You *do*?"

"Sure thing." His eyes are round and blinking. Something in them says, "Why *wouldn't* I swap books with her?" Mine must be saying, "But *how*?" Are they buddies or something?

I make a mad dash for the boarding zone. In the crowded hall, I spy Belinda up ahead, jostling between clumps of kids. The buses are already lined up, motors grumbling and tailpipes belching blue exhaust. Before she gets on her bus, I snag her. "Hey, are you friends with Sam McCorkle?"

"Yep. We've known each other since way back when."

"Back when-when?"

"Since kindergarten. My folks and his folks still get together sometimes." Then she wiggles her eyebrows.

"Makes me wonder why you're asking." I blush, and she grins all the bigger. "I know plenty of stuff about him, for your information."

"You do? Like what?"

"That's for me to know and you to find out."

"Oh, come on, give me a hint!" But it's no use. I get nothing but eyebrow wiggles. "I know: he likes Abigail, doesn't he?" I say.

She claps a hand over her mouth and dies laughing. "Wrong! Wrong, Peewee! You're not as smart as you think!"

★21★
THE PENCIL

Ricky takes the seat next to me and starts playing keep-away with a fifth-grader across the aisle. "That's my pencil!" the kid says. "Give it back!"

Ricky cackles. "It's mine now!"

"No, it's not!"

Denise, my usual seatmate, is headed toward us down an aisle crowded with book bags and feet and band instruments. Once the bus gets in gear, she starts sliding. Ricky leaps up and snatches her ponytail. "Let go of me!" she shrieks.

"Come on, baby, let's sit together." By together, he means squeezed between him and me like a piece of bologna between two slices of Wonder Bread.

"Quit it!" Denise screeches. "You're not my boyfriend, and you never will be!" She pulls away and keeps moving.

"Ouch. You really know how to hurt a guy."

The bus bumps over the pothole and makes its way around to the street, where it picks up speed. Now the boy across the aisle whines, "Can I pleeeease have my pencil back?"

The driver yells, "You, big kid—give that boy his pencil!"

"Here, whiny baby." Ricky tosses the pencil to the boy and then hunches over his book bag, chewing his nails. After a while, he mutters sideways at me, "I told my cousin Tina about you."

Now he's got my attention. "What for?"

"So she can lick her chops about Field Day."

"Humph. If she even exists." I'm not about to show him I'm scared.

"You calling me a liar?"

"Somebody told me you like to cook up whoppers."

He scowls. "They're wrong! Tina's real, and I'm going to prove it to you. You'll be sorry, too, because when she gets here, you're dead meat!"

"That's what you think." I even fake a yawn. But I'm starting to worry that Ricky could be telling the truth. If he is, I *will* be dead meat. I'll be plastered flatter than a sausage patty, unless I get serious about running. Real serious.

He jabs me in the shoulder. "You're quaking in your boots, aren't you? Or whatever South Americans wear."

"Shut up! You don't know a blooming thing about South Americans!"

"I know they're dark-headed spinach speakers." There's a mocking glint in his eyes.

"You mean Spanish?"

"No, I said *spinach*, and I meant *spinach*. Because whenever I hear somebody speak it, I want to barf." I roll my eyes, but he keeps going. "Yep, Tina's going to squash you flat like an angilada, or whatever y'all call it down yonder in spinach land."

"Enchiladas are Mexican, doofus. I'm from Argentina."

"Same difference. Y'all are all spinach talkers."

"What an ignoramus." I bet you a dollar to a doughnut that Ricky couldn't find South America on a map if it was lit up in neon.

"Hey, I saw you at the Wallace rally the other night." He jabs my arm. "Don't deny it—I saw you!"

"So what? I was just there for the cakewalk."

"Good one!" He puts on a little-girl voice. "*I was just there for the cakewalk.* Isn't your sister a Brewer person?" I don't answer. The bus sways over a speed bump. I'm figuring up how many blocks till my bus stop. Too many. I just might blow a gasket before then.

★ 22 ★
ELECTION DAY

"In today's primary, there are seven candidates for governor. Let's name them." Hands shoot up all over the room, and Miss Garrett starts to list our answers on the chalkboard. While she talks, my eyes turn to the window. Sixth-period PE is in session. I watch the lead group of runners until they disappear from view, which doesn't take long—they're running wide open. I guess they don't know about saving something for the distance.

Miss Garrett's chalk taps the number seven. "Who can name the last candidate?"

At first, nobody says a word. *I* sure can't think of his name; he's one of those candidates most people have never heard of. Finally, Belinda raises her hand. "Coleman Brown!"

"Excellent," Miss Garrett says, which makes Belinda glow and me glow with her.

"Right on, sister!" Charles says. "Give her an A-plus, teacher." Miss Garrett smiles and shakes her head at this, but Charles just keeps on yapping. "Come on, y'all. Power to the people!" Smiling big, he raises his fist in the Black Power salute.

Wouldn't you know it? Nick can't let this slide by. He hops up from his desk so fast that a book goes *bam* on the floor, making the flowers in Miss Garrett's vase quiver. "Don't y'all start that mess in here!" he barks. Lots of white people hate that salute. Two medalists in the 1968 Olympics got in big trouble for making it.

Miss Garrett whirls around. "Nick, hush!"

"I'm not going to hush till he does." He points at Charles.

"You trying to tell us what to do?" Charles says. "Puh-leez. Those days are long gone."

"Preach!" Willa says.

"Long gone?" Nick says. "You wish!" Ugh. I want to shut my ears. This reminds me too much of the Wallace rally.

Now the whole class starts rumbling and sniping. In no time, Charles is out of his desk and leaning over mine, in the direction of Nick.

"You want to make something of it?" Nick says.

I cower down in my seat, while the two boys' faces nearly

meet over my head. Charles's eyes flash at Nick's, and Nick's eyes flash at Charles's. They're like dogs circling each other before a fight. And look who's slapdab in the middle: *me*! Isn't Miss Garrett going to do anything? Normally, she would've headed for the light switch by now, but I guess she's like me—paralyzed.

Then I hear Spider: "Take it easy, y'all. Let's just be cool, dig?" For once, he's not joking or being a goof. After a few more seconds of flashing eyes, the boys drop back to their own desks. Whew. And you never saw Miss Garrett looking so grateful. After this, Spider's got himself an A-plus in social studies—I bet you anything.

"Let's return to the lesson, please." Miss Garrett's voice shakes a little, and I don't wonder. "What's a majority?" She writes a percentage sign on the board. "And what happens if no candidate receives at least fifty-one percent of the vote?"

Hands go up. "A runoff."

She explains that if there is a runoff, it will happen four weeks from now, on June 2. But I can barely hear what she's saying. My eyeballs stay on high alert for the least movement between Charles and Nick. Maybe fur didn't fly *this* time, but guess who's getting caught up in the tussle if they go fisticuffs for real? Me, the girl in the middle.

★ 23 ★
THE RETURNS

Our TV isn't picking up squat, and Mamá can't fix it. "Call your father at work. I've got to stay at this sewing machine."

But Papá has too many repairs to finish. "Have you tried tilting the antenna in different directions?" he says.

"Yes, sir, a bunch of times. I get nothing but static."

"Hm. It's probably the weather."

"But I have to watch election returns—it's my homework!"

"Ask Mamá to call the Sampredos. You can watch it over there."

Lucky for me, Mrs. Sampredo tells Mamá it's fine. I grab an umbrella and dash across the street. Mrs. Sampredo plumps up the sofa cushions and turns on the television for me. Their TV is way nicer than ours. No static, no wavy lines—you can see everything clearly. All three channels are broadcasting the returns, so I just pick one, while Mrs. Sampredo settles into the recliner and props her feet up. I can't help but notice her silky Chinese slippers because Marina suggested we get Mamá new bedroom slippers for Mother's Day. I wish we could get some as fancy as those.

I start off writing down almost everything the announcers say, stuff about what time the polls closed and what the turnout was like. I ask Mrs. Sampredo if she wants me to translate, but she says no, since she has to pick up her husband at work pretty soon. Fifteen minutes pass, and the vote tally barely budges. The announcers keep repeating themselves about how many precincts have reported. Blah blah blah. Surely I don't have to write down *everything*.

The newspaper is lying on the coffee table. I check the sports pages, where maybe, just maybe, I'll spot Tina Briggs's name. Nope. Then I read the comic strips and scan the store ads. At Landon's Department Store, lady things are on sale, including Dearfoams slippers. They're not fancy-schmancy like Mrs. Sampredo's, but the ad claims they're silky soft, and they come in blue, which Mamá would love to pieces. I figure Marina and I better hurry over there to buy them.

After Mrs. Sampredo leaves to pick up Mr. Sampredo, I

dial Abigail's house. She snatches up the receiver in a flash. "Whoa, you must've had the phone in your hand," I say.

"I'm expecting a call any minute!" She sounds out of breath. "Long distance!"

"From who, your brother?" He's off in the army, at a post somewhere in California.

"Lordy, would I be sitting by the phone for *him*?"

"Well, who is it then?"

"Guess!" she says.

"Uh. Let's see . . . long distance. Katya?"

"Nope."

"Irina or somebody else from the international club?"

"Nope, this is even better!" She sounds positively giddy.

"Okay, I give up."

"Conrad! Conrad Mays!"

"You mean Phyllis's cousin? Why in the Sam Hill is he calling *you*?"

"Don't say it like that! He asked Phyllis if *I* was going to the party—me, little old me!" Conrad Mays is a hotshot from Mississippi who comes to visit his Alabama relations now and then. Last year at the sock hop, the boys in our class acted like the dance floor might electrocute them, but ole Conrad swept in and danced with nearly every girl. Naturally, this led to some of them falling in love.

I lower the TV volume to zero. "Aren't you watching the election returns?"

But she cuts in kind of quick. "I better get off the phone so I won't miss his call!"

"Okay. Bye." The sound on the TV is still off, but the numbers on the display board behind the news desk haven't changed much. I have half a mind to dial up Belinda to see what she's doing, but here come the Sampredos.

Mrs. Sampredo sets a plate for me, but I tell her I've already had supper. After they eat, Mr. Sampredo pulls out his pipe. "Brewer has the lead, huh? That's good. Better for everybody if he wins. Why didn't your sister come over to watch?"

"She's watching at the Brewer campaign with the other volunteers."

"And you don't volunteer?"

"Not really. I'm not old enough."

Mrs. Sampredo wants to know where's my friend, the nice girl who went with us to Birmingham. I tell her she's at home. I don't bother explaining that right about now, Abigail's probably drooling over every word that falls out of Conrad's mouth.

When Papá arrives, Mrs. Sampredo offers us coffee and snacks. She sets out her dainty espresso cups and frilly napkins. Papá tells funny stories about today's customers.

Now and then, I glance at the TV to see if anything

exciting is going on at the news desk. Never happens. To pass the time, I munch on crackers with guava paste that the Sampredos brought from their last trip to Miami. Pretty tasty. Mrs. Sampredo always talks about moving to Miami, since that's where lots of Cubans live, but for some reason it hasn't happened yet. I hope it never does, or Mamá would lose her best friend.

Papá glances at my notebook on the coffee table. "Aren't you taking notes?"

I shrug. "Not anymore. It's slower than Christmas."

They drink cup after cup of coffee and swap stories about Cuba and Argentina, which I always love hearing. Mrs. Sampredo says, "I wish Claudia could be here with us!"

"She's busy on that bride's dress," Papá says. "You know how she is, nothing short of perfection will do." He sets his coffee cup on the tray. "It's getting late. Have you seen enough of the returns, Lu? I don't think you're even watching."

"I tried, but nothing ever happens," I say. "And anyway, the morning paper will have the final results."

We cross the intersection under the streetlight. When a breeze stirs the May leaves, raindrops wink.

"I sure hope Brewer gets enough votes to avoid a runoff," Papá says.

"Me too." Actually, that's what I try to say, but a giant yawn eats my words.

★24★
GIVE PEACE A CHANCE

Today, I wake up to find out that Governor Brewer didn't get enough votes in the election, meaning there's going to be a runoff between him and Wallace. Nope, I don't blame Marina for being down in the mouth. That gloomy cloud follows me all the way to school, and when the bus stops to pick up Ricky, I'm relieved that he sits far away. I couldn't stand hearing any of his smart-aleck comments this morning.

In homeroom, Abigail is at her desk, in a frenzy to finish schoolwork. "I stayed up late talking to Conrad and forgot to do my definitions." She twists a strand of hair and shoots me a guilty grin. For the first time, I notice blond streaks running through her light-brown hair.

"Are you starting on Nordic Gold already?"

"Lu, I don't have time to talk!"

Oh, brother. Next thing you know, she'll get false eyelashes or something, and I'll look even more behind the times next to her. Abigail claims romance is supposed to happen at boy-girl parties, but *how*, if I look like a fourth-grader? If I brought it up, though, Abigail would probably force me to read those *Groovy Gal* magazines. "Lu," she'd say, "there's a whole education under your bed, and you're letting spiderwebs grow all over it!" She doesn't get it. Mamá would never let me do glamour stuff on myself.

Sam slides into his desk. "What did your sister think about the election?"

"Uh . . . she's not a happy camper."

"Me neither." He unzips his book bag and lays his fountain pen and notebook on the desk. "So do you ever hang around at the campaign offices?"

"Just that once. Do you?"

"Most every time my parents go. I like it over there." He flips the notebook over. "But I guess you've got your running to worry about."

"How did you know about that?"

"I see you from the band room."

"Oh." Now I'm the one blinking. "Do you ever run?"

"Nah. I'm more of a music person than a sports person."

"I love music, too!"

"Yeah? Like which bands?" Those gray eyes are fixed on me and—*eek!*—my mind goes into a spin. "The Beatles?" he says, trying to be helpful.

"Heck, yeah!"

He shows me the back cover of the notebook, where it says, in neat block letters, GIVE PEACE A CHANCE. "This song has my favorite lyrics, but for the sound, I prefer most anything on the *Sgt. Pepper's* album."

Next to GIVE PEACE A CHANCE, there's a cartoony picture of a dove and a guitar. "Wow, did you draw that?" I ask.

"Yep. I wanted to express my feelings about the war in Vietnam and stuff." Red creeps up his neck, and he blinks a jillion times. I watch while he fiddles with the drawing, adding more lines to the dove's wings.

"You're good!"

He shrugs. "Not that good, but I try." He looks up and smiles. I think bumblebees are flying around inside my head.

The bell goes *claaaaaang*, and Mrs. Donnelly scurries in to start the day. Dang it, just when Sam and I finally broke out of our shyness and really got to talking. While Mrs. Donnelly writes stuff on the chalkboard, it finally dawns on me how I should've answered his question. Sly and the Family Stone is pretty much my favorite band now, but "Brown Eyed Girl" by Van Morrison is the song I love most. Maybe I can tell him later.

Golly, Sam talked to me! *Really* talked! A bubble of happiness practically lifts me out of my desk. The day goes by with me riding that bubble. Then in sixth period, the election quiz lands on my desk. There are ten questions.

Number one: "Did any candidate for governor receive a majority of votes?" No. That was easy-peasy.

Number two: "What is a precinct?" I drum my pencil on my chin. *Precinct* sounds familiar, but I can't exactly define it. I'll come back to this question later. The answers to three, four, five, seven, and ten roll off my ballpoint pen in a flash. But number six stops me in my tracks and number nine really throws me for a loop: "Name the call letters of the television station you used for watching the election returns." Whaaat? Nobody ever pays attention to call letters—you just turn on the TV and flip channels till you find your program. I rub my arms and stare at the blank spaces.

Miss Garrett says, "Five minutes." I hear Sam's fountain pen scratching away. The second hand on the wall clock is red, and the red hand shows that time is flying. Red's also the color of Miss Garrett's grading pen, the pen that slashes Xs across wrong answers. That pen has never written anything but A-pluses on *my* test papers. Seven out of ten is 70 percent, and Lu Olivera doesn't make C-minuses!

Two minutes. I scribble guesses on numbers six and nine, and hurry back to the one about precincts. I *should* know this. It was all over the returns last night, but reaching for the answer is like trying to grab Ringo when he doesn't want to be grabbed. Then Miss Garrett announces, "Time's up. Pass your quizzes forward."

There are groans across the classroom. I turn around, and Sam's sticking his fountain pen in his pocket. "How'd you do?" I ask him.

"Pretty good, I think." He blinks those gray eyes and smiles a shy one.

"You knew all that stuff about precincts?"

"Sure. They said it every other minute last night. Didn't you watch the returns?"

I frown. "Of course."

On the bus, we edge around the school driveway in bumper-to-bumper traffic. For the first time in ages, I'm not daydreaming about running. Lu, you messed up. You blew that quiz. And now Sam thinks you're a total dummy who doesn't have the foggiest idea what a precinct is.

★25★
EXTRA CREDIT

The next day in PE, something's wrong. It's like my battery is on the blink and I've forgotten how to run. Although I pump my arms and legs with everything I've got, huffing and puffing, wishing and praying, I've got no speed today.

Madeline Manning, are you there? No answer. All I get is the *trill, trill, peep, peep, chortle, chortle* of mockingbirds as I shuffle around the driveway like a little old lady on crutches. Meanwhile, Angie blasts around the final curve at rocket speed, with Belinda not far behind. When I finally reach the chalk line, a hundred years later, Mrs. Underwood has the saddest of faces. "Olivera, what happened to your giddyap and go?" I wish I knew how to answer that.

It gets worse. In the locker room, Missy says, "Somebody forgot to eat their Wheaties!"

"Good one, Missy!" Phyllis says.

Loser Olivera, that's what they think I am, and today it feels true.

I reach into my purse for a comb and rake it over my porcupine quills. Even worse than what Missy said is Phyllis agreeing with her. Jeez, why did she turn against me? Meanwhile, Abigail's in front of the mirror, fluffing her hair and not saying boo. Maybe she didn't hear Missy. Or maybe she's pretending that she didn't.

Then comes social studies, where all it takes is seeing Miss Garrett, with her fingers clenched around her grade book, to figure out that we're in for it. There are moans all over the place when she hands out our graded quizzes. I turn mine over carefully, curling the corners of the paper so nobody else can see. In bloodred ink, there it is: a big, fat C-minus. I feel faint.

Sam got a one hundred on his quiz. I caught sight of his paper when she laid it on his desk.

In a huffy voice, Miss Garrett says, "I'm appalled at these grades. I have to wonder if you all really and truly watched the election returns. How disappointing." Her eyes go straight to me when she says this, and I think I might die. She continues. "I've decided to offer extra credit. But it won't be a walk in the park. You'll have to write me a report on something related to the election. The worse your grade, the more effort you need to put in." Kids stir in their seats and start chattering. "Hush," she says in a sharp voice that makes everybody freeze. "Be grateful for this chance and get to work."

Paige raises her hand. "But what can we write about exactly?"

"Fair question. Those of you who attended the Wallace rally have an excellent topic."

At the same time that Willa lets out a gasp, Spider says, "For *real*?"

"Hang on, Miss Garrett!" Charles says. "That's discrimination!"

"Why, Charles? Wallace is the only candidate that held a rally here. If you didn't go, just write a report on something else. Stop being obstinate." She looks crosser than a cross-eyed bear.

Charles shakes his head firmly. "No, ma'am. You said it's an excellent topic, but you know us black kids wouldn't go to no stinking Wallace rally!"

Miss Garrett snaps, "Charles, would you like to go see Mr. Abrams?"

"Send him!" Nick says.

"Nick!" Miss Garrett's eyes are drop-dead serious. "I won't

113

stand for your disruptions either!" Suddenly it's quiet as a graveyard. The vase on her desk is full of black-eyed Susans with friendly little faces, but Miss Garrett doesn't look so friendly today.

When the bell rings, we practically tiptoe out of there.

Sam stops me to ask if I plan to drop by campaign head-quarters today. I tell him I'll have to check with my mom, but this is a total fib. I can't waste a minute of time today. I've got to park myself at the kitchen table for as long as it takes to write the best report on a political rally that Miss Garrett has ever seen.

The Red Grove Gazette

CAMPUS PROTESTS ERUPT

★ 26 ★

ASSEMBLY

The newspaper is spread open on the breakfast table. A big antiwar protest broke out yesterday at our state university, and I'm stuck here listening to Papá and Marina argue about it. Poor Mamá isn't any happier than I am. She stirs her tea and sighs.

"You're wrong, hija," Papá says. "A civil society requires order. If you ask me, Governor Brewer did the right thing in siding with the police, not the protestors, who ought to be more worried about their studies than anything else."

Marina says, "Papá, come on! This is a matter of freedom of speech! It's why we have a First Amendment!" While Papá and Marina go back and forth with law-and-order this, freedom-of-speech that, Mamá and I exchange a look. We both sigh. I know Papá's not against people having their say. He just doesn't agree with the way the university students did it. Jeez, it sure gives me the willies to hear my family squabble. Don't I get enough of that at school, between Nick and Charles? Now my eggs taste like plastic.

Mamá follows me out to the sidewalk as I head for the bus. "Don't worry, hija," she says. "Your sister knows better than to get mixed up with protests." I can just about read her mind: *We're foreigners. We're not supposed to get involved.*

"I know, Mamá." I plant a kiss on her cheek and make a dash for the corner, where the bus has just pulled up.

Me and Mamá, we're birds of a feather. Worry birds.

At the end of homeroom, the school intercom comes alive with a crackle: "Assembly commences in fifteen minutes." We hurry along the covered walkway to the high school, and then to the very back of the auditorium, which is where we lowly sixth-graders have to sit.

Abigail plops down next to me. "Look at what came in the mail." She shoves a postcard in my hand. "It's from Conrad!" There's just one line, written in the worst chicken scratch: *See you at Phyllis's big bash.—Conrad.* Not too personal, if you ask me, but I don't want to burst Abigail's balloon. And anyway, what do *I* know about boys? Zero.

Mr. Abrams is at the lectern. "Final exam schedules go out on Monday. Teachers will distribute them in homeroom."

Next, Mr. Barkley gives a talk about science fairs. Then Mrs. Underwood explains what to expect on Field Day. She reminds teachers they'll have events, too, which makes us kids laugh, because did you ever see teachers trying to do sports?

My mind wanders and so do my eyes, flitting across hairdos and hair bows sticking up over the tops of the auditorium seats. Belinda is two rows up. I spot her by her ponytail.

Abigail whispers, "Have you chosen your outfit for the party yet?"

"No, have you?"

"Sure have. I'm going to Birmingham to get myself white bell-bottoms from Pizitz. Daddy raised my allowance."

"Ooh, nice!"

"You should get your parents to raise yours, too."

"Very funny. You know my parents. I'd have to do extra chores." Not that doing extra chores would help me much. After all, Mamá is saving every penny for her trip to Argentina.

The whole auditorium is rustling and whispering now. Once the program winds down, the high-school kids start filing out first. Our turn won't come for eons.

Abigail has more advice. "You'd better start thinking about Phyllis's birthday gift, too."

"Already? The party's not for weeks."

"Lu! Get your head screwed on straight! How are y'all going to be friends again unless she believes you still care?"

"Are you bonkers? Missy would never let Phyllis be my friend again!"

"Don't forget that Missy's going to East Lake next year."

"Phyllis probably will, too."

"Her parents haven't decided yet. I overheard her and Missy talking. And you know what else I overheard? They think you like Sam!" She gives me a sideways look. "I figured you don't, or you would've already told me—right?"

"Well." I pause. "I *could* like him, but only if I found out he likes me back."

She lets out a squeal. "Lu, why didn't you tell me, you little ninny?" Then she grabs my arm. "The party—that's where you'll find out for sure if he likes you! Haven't I been telling you this? I bet he'll ask you to dance. That's why you've got to get your outfit planned! You need something groovy. Something mod."

"I don't have anything groovy or mod."

"Then you've got to go shopping, silly!"

The auditorium is almost empty. We slowly make our way toward the exit. Abigail doesn't get it. What I wear to the party will be something handmade by Mamá. It'll be perfectly stitched, all right, but you can bet your sweet bippy it won't be groovy or mod.

★ 27 ★
LANDON'S

Marina is yanking laundry off the clothesline. She hands me one edge of a bedsheet and we shake it a few times. *Pop. Pop.* The sheet bubbles out and catches the breeze. "I need you to go to Landon's to get those slippers for Mamá before they sell out. Mother's Day is this weekend."

"By myself?"

"Why not? There's nothing to it. Just get those Dearfoams we saw in the ad."

We meet in the middle with our corners. "But whenever Mamá sends me on errands, I can never find what I'm supposed to buy."

"Good grief, don't act all helpless with me. I have papers to write."

"Okay, okay." I take a stack of sheets in my arms and head for the back door. Shopping: I could murder it. But what I hate even worse than shopping is crossing Marina when she's in a testy mood.

"Lu, keep it quiet in there," she calls after me. "Mamá's got a headache."

While I put the laundry away, a new thought comes to me. I know what else I can do on this shopping trip: look for Phyllis's present. Something extra cool, just like Abigail suggested, something to make her remember what good friends we used to be.

When I get to the store, my worst prediction has come true: Dearfoams bedroom slippers in Mamá's size are gone, sold out! Didn't I tell Marina this would happen? Now I've got to figure out something else to get. Sure, there are other slippers, but they're not as nice as the ones Marina and I decided on. I roam the store looking for other ideas. There are Mother's Day displays everywhere—fondue pots, spray colognes, lacy handkerchiefs with fancy monograms—but nothing seems right for Mamá. After tearing around in a tizzy, I circle back to the shoe department. One of these other brands of slippers will have to do. I look high and low and finally find a pair in baby blue, size six. At least they're on sale.

Now for Phyllis's gift. A saleslady asks, "Can I help you find something, hon?" I explain that I need a birthday gift for a girl my age. "Oh, we've got scads of stuff for girls." Her syrupy smile makes her eyes crinkle. "I'd start in the accessories department."

In the hats and scarves section, two ladies are at the mirror, trying on beach hats. Sixth-graders don't wear stuff like that. Scarves neither. This is old-people stuff.

When you get down to it, everything about Landon's is old-timey. The floor is made of planks that go *creak*. The ceilings are about twenty feet high, and the light fixtures that hang from them are dim on account of forty years' worth of dust. And Mr. Landon, who I've seen wandering the aisles sometimes, fits right into this place. He's somewhere around two hundred, and a stiff wind could blow him clear to the next county.

Somebody taps my shoulder. "Hi, you." It's Belinda. She's carrying a blue shopping bag that could only be from Myron's, the bookstore.

"Hi, yourself. What you got there, more books?"

"It's a Mother's Day present. My mom, she eats up books." I guess that's where Belinda gets it from.

"So does my sister."

Belinda cocks her head at me. "So what're you doing here?"

"I just paid for my mom's gift. Now I'm looking for a birthday present for a girl our age. There's this party I have to go to."

Belinda lifts an eyebrow. "Weird! I never heard of *having* to go to a party."

"It's for somebody that's kind of a friend and kind of not. I better not say who, but I need something extra good." I'm not about to explain to Belinda what's been going on with Phyllis, Missy, and Loser Olivera. Or blab about a party she's not even invited to!

Belinda doesn't ask any more questions about that. "Well, earrings are always cool. Does she have pierced ears?"

After searching the jewelry racks, we decide there's not a pair of cute earrings in this store. Or bracelets. Or necklaces. In the bargain bins, though, we dig up a plastic wallet with zippered compartments. It's hot pink, very mod, and just what I'd love for myself. But then I notice a tear in the plastic—dang it!

A few minutes later, Belinda comes up with a green purse made of imitation alligator hide. It has a long, adjustable strap and silvery buckles. "Ooh, let me see that!" I sling the strap over my shoulder and twirl around a couple of times. *This* will do it. This is *the* perfect gift!

But then I check the price tag. Rats! The purse isn't on sale, and I don't have enough money.

Belinda can see from my face what the problem is. "Come on, Peewee. Don't get mopey on me." She shoves me in the direction of hair accessories. There are two revolving racks loaded with barrettes, combs, ponytail holders, and headbands. "We're going to find something here—I just know it," she says.

And bingo, there it is: a headband that matches the alligator-hide purse to a T!

We're both smitten. Belinda even says, "Mind if I try it on?" She wiggles her ponytail holder off and lets her hair loose, then smooths it down with both hands. Then she slips the headband around her neck and cinches it to the top of her hairdo. I peek from behind while she checks herself in the mirror.

"Wow," I say. "That's beautiful on you!"

"This is for Phyllis, isn't it?"

"How did you know?"

"You said she was a kind-of friend. You want her back on your side, don't you?" She slips the headband off and hands it to me. "Get both of them—the purse, too. I'll loan you money."

"Nooooo, I can't let you do that!"

"You can't stop me." She stuffs a five-dollar bill in my pocket. I whip it out and stuff it in *her* pocket. With grins on our faces, we "squabble" for a few minutes until I give in.

I'm counting on there being enough quarters in my piggy bank to pay her back, although it might take extra chores and a loan from Marina, too. But when Phyllis sees this gift, it'll be worth it.

On our way to the cash register, we pass the misses' dress department, where I spot two prissy mannequins wearing summery dresses and holding straw purses. One of them has a reddish-brown wig styled in a flip. "Does she remind you of Miss Garrett?" I ask.

"Sure does," Belinda says. But then she takes a closer look. "What's wrong with her hands? The fingertips are all crumbly!"

"Something's been chewing on them. I bet rats are all over this store, come nighttime."

"Eww! I hope not!"

"Nah, they're just old as dirt, like the rest of this store," I say. "Hey, I've got an idea." I lead her over to a display of gloves. We sneak two pairs back to the mannequins. No saleslady or customer is looking in our direction—we make sure of that. I slip a pair of Sunday whites on one manne-quin's hands, while Belinda puts long, silky evening gloves on "Miss Garrett." We giggle nonstop.

Soon, Mr. Landon's rickety voice comes over the PA sys-tem: "The store is closing in ten minutes."

"Oops, better go pay for your stuff," Belinda says.

I hurry toward the cash register and set the headband and purse on the counter. It's the same saleslady as before, only now her syrupy smile is wiped clean off. "Well, well. I've been standing here waiting for you." Heart attack! She saw us with the mannequins! But she jerks a thumb toward Belinda, who's poking around in a rack of pantsuits. "Is that her? The one you're buying this headband for?"

"No, ma'am. She just helped me pick it out. Why?" I chew my lip.

"She tried it on, that's why. Stuck it on her head. I was watching y'all." The way she holds the headband by the edges, you'd think it was a snake. Oh, Lord, I'm finally catching on, and it's a scary, sinking feeling, like quicksand under my feet. She flings the headband into a shopping bag. "If I was you, I wouldn't give it to nobody else after she wore it. But you do as you will."

My heart hammers. How can anybody on God's green earth be so mean? "Ma'am?" I hear myself say, in a teensy, breathless voice. The lady barely glances up, and somehow, much to my surprise, I keep going, because this is my *friend* she's talking so mean about. "Excuse me, ma'am, but that's kind of—uh—rude."

"I beg your pardon!" She slams the drawer of the cash register. "The store is *closed*," she says in a loud, irritated voice.

Belinda is too far away to hear anything—or at least I hope she is. I make like a bullet for the door. Out on the sidewalk, Belinda jerks me to a stop. "What was that woman saying?"

"Nothing." My ears go *thrum-thrum* with a sped-up pulse.

"Didn't look like 'nothing' to me."

I shrug. "She was crabby because of . . . Mr. Landon."

Belinda narrows her eyes at me. "Humph. I could've sworn . . ."

"Thanks for the loan—you're a lifesaver! I'll pay you back on Monday." I pray my chirpy voice will squeeze a smile out of her, but no such luck. Golly bum, I hope she's not mad at *me* now.

★28★
EL CHEAPOS

Marina is in the kitchen, stapling flyers. In a furious whisper, she says, "What in the thunder took you so long? I was at the point of calling Papá!"

"What for? I was shopping, like you asked me to!"

"You took forever! I have enough on my mind without having to worry about you."

"Jeez, you're not my mother!" The nerve of her to send me on a shopping trip and now give me a hard time about it!

"Shh, keep your voice down. Mamá has a bad headache."

"Oops. I forgot."

She glances at the kitchen clock. "They're expecting me at the campaign. It's going to be another long night."

"How come?"

"Because every voter in the county needs to be contacted before the runoff." And here I thought she might be giving up on Brewer after the antiwar protest, but I'm sure she can't forget that Wallace is far worse. She sets the stapler down. "Let me see the slippers."

"Okay, but the Dearfoams were all gone." I'm suddenly nervous that she won't like the ones I picked out.

And I'm right. When she opens the shoe box, her face falls. "Oh, Lu, what happened?"

"They sold out! I had to get a different kind!"

She slaps a hand to her forehead. "Now I've got to come up with something else for Mother's Day!"

"Are you kidding me? There's no more money!"

"No, I'm not kidding! These are El Cheapos! If you want to give them to her, be my guest, but leave me out of it." Boy, she sounds like she could bite somebody's head off. Now I feel like bawling my eyes out. She shoves the stapled flyers into a tote bag, and I blink back tears.

After a long sigh, Marina says, "Lu, I shouldn't have snapped at you. No excuse, but I've had a horrible day."

"That's okay. Mine was sort of horrible, too." I'd like to tell her about Belinda and the saleslady, but I stop myself. She'd throw a conniption fit about justice and stuff. "Go ahead. I'll check on Mamá while you're gone."

"That's very sweet of you. Thanks, Lu."

After she leaves, a stack of mail catches my eye. Along with the ho-hum stuff, there's an unopened letter from Argentina, addressed in my grandmother's handwriting. Strange that Mamá didn't rip it open the second it arrived. I tiptoe to the master bedroom and listen at the door. I knock softly and push it ajar. Mamá's stretched out on the bed with a towel covering her eyes and an ice bag on her forehead. She reaches for my hand. "Mi amor," she whispers.

"Hi, Mamá. Are you going to be okay?" She nods and pats my hand. "Here's a letter from Abuelita," I add. "You didn't open it."

"My eyes hurt too much. Will you read it to me?" It's slow going because I'm not so good at reading Spanish, but it's nice to hear all the things Abuelita writes about our cousins and aunts and uncles. She even mentions her little dog, Fifi, who goes to the market with her every morning. Mamá interrupts my reading. "I don't know what you'll eat for supper."

"We'll manage. Just stay here and rest." I prop the letter on her dresser.

"I can't rest much longer. The dress . . ." Her eyes go to the closet, where the wedding dress hangs, zipped up in a garment bag. Today no sewing got done, and the deadline is getting close.

Pobre Mami. Her rosary is on the dresser, hanging from a pedestal. I unhook it and slip it into her hand. "Maybe you need this."

She smiles. It's just a tiny smile, but it makes me feel better.

In the kitchen, the appliances stare at me with cold steel faces. I'm starving, and nobody is fixing supper. There's a tub of pimento cheese in a back corner of the refrigerator, begging for somebody to notice it. Your wish is granted, pimento cheese. I slop spoonfuls of it on crackers.

An hour later, I'm at the kitchen table fiddling with my corkboard when Papá comes in, carrying a bucket of fried chicken and a bag from the pharmacy. It's Mamá's medicine.

"What a day! Seems like the whole town needed something repaired." He sets the bags down and loosens his tie. "Want some chicken? There's mashed potatoes and cole-slaw, too."

"No, thank you. I'm not that hungry."

He pauses to get a better look at the corkboard. "What's this? Something for school?"

"No, sir, this is just—I don't know—stuff I like."

"Oh? In that case, let's see what kind of stuff Lu likes." I feel a blush coming on. He chuckles at a crinkled picture of Van Morrison that I stuck on the board. It's the only one of

131

him I could find, in a beat-up magazine Marina was throwing out. Then the sports-page clipping catches his eye. "Ah, Madeline Manning. I'd forgotten all about her."

"She got a gold at the Olympics."

"I know, but I'm amazed *you* remember her, after all this time."

"I really like running, that's why."

"Well, you've got a mighty long wait till the next Olympics comes on TV—two years."

"That's not what I meant, Papá . . ." I'm trying to figure out how to say it, that it's not only *watching* track events that I care about, it's doing it, for real, with my feet, not just my eyes. But all at once, it feels like a whole bunch of nervous bees let loose inside my head. All I can think about is how stern Papá got the night they caught me racing at the international club, even though that's not how his eyes look right now. "I mean, you know—*I* like doing running—me."

"Is that a fact? Let me take these pills to your mother. We can talk about it later." After he leaves, the nervous bees start to settle down a little, figuring Papá will be back in a few minutes to talk. But a long time goes by without the door opening at all. Maybe Mamá is feeling worse. That gets the bees stirred up again. Scary bees.

And to think, all I got her were some stupid El Cheapos.

★29★
THE CEMETERY

At the playground, Belinda and I stow our bikes in the azaleas and start our Saturday run. The toughest part is the big bad hill. Every time I tackle it, my leg muscles moan and groan and my ticker pounds like it's going out of style. But we can't slack off. Field Day is coming.

"I bet the girls"—*huff huff*—"from County aren't"—*huff huff*—"running up hills," Belinda says. Every time we reach the top, we walk in circles to catch our breath. A few minutes later, off we go, down the hill and back up.

Afterward, we're a couple of good-for-nothing rag dolls who flop down on our behineys on the playground swings. We laugh at squirrels that chase each other around tree trunks and dive from one branch to the next.

Then Belinda says, "Hey, I want to show you where *I* like to go sometimes."

"Okay!" I don't even ask where.

We hop on our bikes and start pedaling. She leads me to the end of the street, where we hook a left. A bunch of corners later, we're in a part of town I've never seen. We pass a beauty salon, a church, a fruit stand, and a corner grocery mart. I follow her through a neighborhood of pink, blue, and yellow houses, where every person on the sidewalk or standing in a yard with a garden hose is black. They wave at us. We wave back. I'm beaming because nobody here seems to think it's strange that two girls, one black and one not, would ride bikes together.

Finally, we come to a big sign that arches over the road. It says OAKWOOD CEMETERY. We drop our bikes by the gatepost and head down the gravel driveway on foot. There are graves all around, but in the plain sunshine, it's not scary at all— it's like a park full of beautiful trees. Belinda skips. I skip behind her. Ahead, there's a tunnel of oak trees that begs for girls like us to run through it. So we do. When we reach the farthest point, we're in a shady cave made of leaves. Birds twitter over our heads, and the smell of honeysuckle is thick as can be. "Gosh, it feels like heaven in here!" I say.

Belinda's grinning. "I knew you'd like it! Come here, let

me show you my favorite part." We reach a park bench tucked under a tall cedar. "This is where I go to read a book sometimes."

"I hope birds don't doo-doo on you."

"Don't jinx it, Peewee."

Then I remember what Marina said about Belinda. "My sister said to bring you by the house. She's got some books you can borrow." I'm sure it's okay to invite her because Mamá woke up feeling all better today.

"Cool!"

We lollygag for the longest time, plucking the ripest honeysuckle blooms we can find and slurping up their tiny drops of sweetness. I decide to tell her about the invitation with "Loser" written on it. She tells me about a friend that did her dirty. I ask her if she likes anybody special, and she says sort of, but he lives in Montgomery and she hasn't seen him since Christmas. "*You* like somebody, don't you?" she says.

"A little bit."

"Well, pretty soon, it's going to be a *lot*!"

"What does that mean?"

"Ha, wouldn't you like to know?" Then she locks her lips with an invisible key and folds her arms across her chest. Begging doesn't work, so I throw acorns at her, but all she does is laugh. We run in circles through bushes and graves, pelting each other with berries and pinecones, till my shirt's sticking to my back and my throat's parched like nobody's business.

"Want to go to Handy's for soda and a snack?"

"Good thinking, Peewee." It being Saturday, most stores close at noon, but Handy's is open all day long. After we get our snacks, we prop our bikes against a lamppost and stroll down the empty streets, mostly window-shopping. By the time we've finished our Dr Peppers, she's got half of her candied peanuts left and I've got half of my Junior Mints. We swap candies and park ourselves on the steps of the courthouse. The bronze Confederate soldiers on the lawn don't seem to care that we're friends, but two old geezers passing by give us nasty looks.

"I hate when people do that," I say.

Belinda eyes me. "Like that saleslady?"

Uh-oh. I feel myself blushing to the roots of my hair. "You heard what she said?"

"Not really, but now you're going to tell me."

"I didn't want you to hear it!"

"Tell me," she says. "Now, Peewee. *Now*." Yesterday on the sidewalk in front of Landon's, her eyes had fiery little sparks in them, and now those sparks are back. So I tell her.

She says, "That's what I figured. Exactly what I figured. I'm never going back to that store."

"Me neither."

"Promise?"

"Promise." We shake pinkies on it.

Belinda stands up. "Come on, I want to see your sister's books!" We grab our bikes and race down Cornelius. When we reach my house, I introduce her to Mamá, who's tacking the hem of the wedding dress with sewing pins. Still, she stops what she's doing and insists on serving us cookies, not that we're the least bit hungry. I'm just happy that Belinda can see how sweet Mamá is, and Mamá can meet my newest friend.

After Belinda chooses some paperbacks from Marina's bookshelves, we stretch out on the rug next to my bed and listen to the radio. I ask her if she thinks Tina Briggs is real, but she's never heard of her either. I tell her about Madeline Manning, and she tells me about Wilma Rudolph, another American gold medalist.

"Know what? Madeline Manning is sort of my running coach."

Belinda sits up and frowns. "Say that again?"

I feel goofy for bringing it up, but Belinda's waiting for my explanation. "Uh. It's kind of like I hear her talking to me—not out loud, but in my head." She looks at me like I'm batty, so I figure I better keep talking. "Sort of. Not for real."

"Me oh my, Peewee. Let me see if you have a fever." She presses a hand to my forehead. "Yep, call the doctor. This girl has stayed out in the sun too long!"

★ 30 ★
MOTHER'S DAY

I take a tray rattling with china and set it down on the table in front of Mamá. Flowers, doilies, pretty teacups. She looks over everything with shining eyes. "Oh, you shouldn't have gone to so much fuss!"

Papá says, "You deserve a fuss, darling! Happy Mother's Day!"

Whew. I was jittery as a polecat getting everything together without Marina. She stayed up all night working on Mamá's present, so it was only right to let her sleep in. She's at the table now, but with big raccoon circles under her eyes.

Mamá is crazy about the fruit salad I made and the coffee cake Papá got from the bakery. She drinks nearly a gallon of hot tea with cream and sugar. That's the easy part. Then Papá announces, "We have a few surprises for you!"

I bite my knuckles. When he hands her the gift-wrapped slippers, she reads my card and eagerly opens the box. "What a lovely blue, just like my robe! Gracias, mi amor!" She plants a kiss on my forehead, then kicks off her faded terry-cloth slippers and swaps them with the new ones. Right next to her robe, you can tell the blues don't match—not by a country mile—but she acts like they're the latest thing from Paris. Whew.

Marina says, "Papá, you go next."

As Mamá peels away the Scotch tape on Papá's gift, her smile is almost as big as the box. She breaks into a laugh when she sees the picture on the carton. It's a Lady Sunbeam hair dryer, the kind that fits over your head like a bonnet.

Marina excuses herself, saying she'll be right back. I know why; it's time to show Mamá the secret project she worked on all night.

"More tea, Mamá?" I ask.

Papá slices the hair-dryer carton open. Getting the dryer out of the box is no easy trick. There are lots of Styrofoam pieces holding it in place, and it takes tugging and prying to set the dryer free. Sitting on the table, it looks enormous. Mamá leans in close while he shows her the adjustments you can make to temperature, fan speed, angle, and who knows what all. "You'll never have to sleep in your curlers again."

Mamá and Papá are still cooing like lovey doves when Marina shows up, carrying the garment bag that holds the wedding dress. Mamá sees it and gasps. "What's wrong?"

"Nothing's wrong. This is my Mother's Day gift to you." Smiling, Marina unzips the bag. The stitches of the finished hem are tiny and perfect, exactly how Mamá would've sewn them herself. At first, Mamá can't even speak.

"Santa Claus's elves paid you a visit last night," Papá says, grinning. "We never knew they worked on Mother's Day."

"Gracias, hija," Mamá says, wiping away tears. "You made my job much easier!"

Ah, what a nice Mother's Day it turned out to be! Now that the wedding dress is nearly finished, Mamá can count on buying a plane ticket to Argentina. I can tell that she's on Cloud Ninety-Nine. She nibbles at the coffee cake, eats an extra serving of fruit salad, and props her slippered feet up on the ottoman next to the couch. All the while, Papá tunes his guitar. "What would you like to hear, Claudia?"

"You don't even need to ask—'Besame Mucho.'"

Oh, brother, things are getting mushier by the minute around here. It's time for me to scram. Monkey bars, here I come.

★31★
ARE WE DREAMING?

Homeroom bell is about to ring. Grinning like a jack-o'-lantern, Abigail whips out a postcard and hands it to me. It's signed *Yours truely, Conrad*—misspelling and all. "We're on the phone every night," she says. "His father's business has a WATS line that you can talk on for hours and hours without paying for long distance."

My jaw drops. "You talk for *hours and hours*?"

"Shhh! Daddy doesn't know how late I've been staying up!" She does a little dance. "I like Conrad! Conrad likes me!"

"No wonder you're always finishing assignments in homeroom."

"Yep. And when he comes to town for the party, it'll be even worse!"

"Jeez, I hope he helps you study for exams."

"Oh, Lu, you're so funny!" Now she whispers. "Don't tell anybody, pleeeeease, but his family's for Wallace."

"Don't they live in Mississippi? Why would they care about Alabama's governor?"

"Oh, they care, all right. People love Wallace, up and down the country. Just don't tell Daddy or he might write my name out of the will!"

"Heck, it's not like you're *marrying* Conrad. You're just going to a party together."

"You never know," she says. "Mama and Daddy were high-school sweethearts."

I'm starting to think Abigail has lost her marbles.

"Something's going on with Connie. She's not even trying to run fast." This is me, whispering to Belinda after we've parked our hindquarters on the curb under the shade of the tulip trees. There's not one iota of breeze stirring, and we're craving air-conditioning like a dog craves a ham bone.

Instead of answering, Belinda cuts her eyes in the direction of Mrs. Underwood, who stands next to us and could be listening. In her giant sunglasses, Mrs. Underwood reminds me of a housefly.

"Mercy me," she says, while scribbling on her clipboard. "I couldn't put a piece of paper between you two at the finish line. Y'all are going to smoke them on Field Day! Wonder what a good track-and-field coach could do with you two. Y'all got real talent that deserves development. So I was talking to Coach Williams and he made an interesting suggestion: summer track clinic at the state university. It's a camp for runners."

Belinda blurts, "Sign *me* up!"

Mrs. Underwood flashes her gold molars. "That's the spirit! We'll talk some more after I get the hard facts. Let me see how Angie and Connie like the idea."

Belinda and I head back to the locker room. "Are we dreaming?" she says. "Pinch me!"

But I don't know what in the dickens to say. While she floats, I'm turning into a nervous Nellie. What would Mamá and Papá say if they heard about this business of track camp? They have no clue that I've been running at all, except for that one little ole race at the international club. And look how well that went over with them: like a lead balloon!

After changing back into my school clothes, I get word that Mrs. Underwood wants to see me in her office. As soon as I push the door open, she starts in. "Olivera, let me shoot it straight. Will you be here next year or are you transferring?"

"I'm staying right here."

"Good. I got to ask because lots of kids are leaving for that private school."

"*Lots* of kids?"

"So says the grapevine. I just need to know if my talented runners are coming back next year. Otherwise, what's the point in trying to put together a track team?" *Track team*? A few minutes ago, she said track camp, and now we've graduated up to *track team*? Belinda will jump for joy when she hears this.

"You've got speed, Olivera. We really need your legs to put together a program. I've got pretty good sprinters in the seventh and eighth grades, but every team needs somebody that can handle distance. That's you, my friend. So get cracking and ask your mom and pop to sign on the dotted line." She hands me a permission form for track camp.

"But what about the other girls?" I ask.

"Belinda's my ace for the four-forty. Angie, she burns it up in the sprints." Mrs. Underwood sighs. "And I'm afraid that ole Connie might be bailing on us. We're losing her to East Lake next year." So that explains why Connie hasn't seemed to care about running lately. She's already got one foot out the door.

Golly, everything's changing so fast. One by one, white kids are kissing this school good-bye. Who's next, I wonder?

145

The first good sign is Miss Garrett's hundred-watt smile. The more she walks down the rows, swishing her yellow skirt and spreading the smell of flowery perfume, the better I feel. She hands me back my report on the Wallace rally, and there, at the top right corner, glows a red A-plus, along with the word *Exceptional*. I'm weak in the knees with relief.

But why, oh why, of all the blooming times it could've happened, does Sam have to peek over my shoulder while I'm holding *this* report?

"You went to the Wallace rally?"

"Not so loud!" Lucky for me, the class is chattering away like a tree full of squirrels. I think fast. "What makes you figure I went?"

"You wrote a report on it!" He does a rapid-fire blink.

"I needed extra credit, remember?"

"Yeah, but you're for Brewer!"

"Of course I am! My sister practically lives at his campaign offices!"

"That's why I thought . . ." he stammers. "But now . . ." More blinking.

Miss Garrett zips over to switch the lights off-on-off-on. It takes a while for us squirrels to settle down. Then she starts checking our election notebooks. When she reaches my desk, she gives my shoulder a squeeze. "Glad to see your work improving, Lu."

When she moves to the next row, I notice Sam's got his fountain pen out, writing down our assignment. He needs to get it through his head that I would never root for Wallace. Going to the rally was supposed to be for a cakewalk, nothing else. "Hey," I whisper to him, "didn't you hear about the cakewalk?"

"Huh? The cake what?"

I'm about to explain when I realize that he looks mighty annoyed, like maybe he thinks cakewalks are the stupidest things ever. If I let on that I went to the rally for something like a cakewalk, he's going to take me for a flighty girl—one who doesn't give a hoot that Wallace is one of the worst racists to come down the turnpike, so long as she can play some dumb ole game with cakes for prizes.

Sam caps the fountain pen and sticks it in his pocket. A little frown between his eyebrows makes me think he's had it with me. When Miss Garrett starts the lesson, my mind is nowhere near social studies. And then, once the last bell of the day rings, Sam up and vanishes without a good-bye or anything. Now I won't see him till tomorrow, and he's gone home thinking I'm a Wallace girl. Oh, crud.

★ 33 ★
THE NOTE

Next day, Sam is back at it. "All I want to know is, did you go or not?"

Mrs. Donnelly dusts chalk off her hands. She has just finished writing today's date, Wednesday, May 13, on the board. "Everyone take a seat, please."

"Well?" Sam says.

"Shhh, class is about to start." My nerves are fried from all these questions. I pull out my language notebook and face the front of the classroom.

While Mrs. Donnelly starts passing out copies of our exam schedule, Sam taps me on the shoulder again. "Can't you just say yes or no, and be done with it?"

I frown. "Hush, we'll get in trouble." In my notebook, I

flip to today's vocabulary list, but Sam won't stop breathing down my neck.

"Yes or no? Simple question." Mrs. Donnelly is calling roll, but Sam acts like that doesn't matter. He just leans in closer and whispers in my ear, "So you're saying yes?"

Barely turning my head, I hiss, "I didn't say that!"

"Then you lied? Writing the report would be a lie if you didn't go!" I just shake my head without uttering a peep, but suddenly it's like the world has come to an end for ole Sam. "Oh, no. You went! I can tell you did. Oh, God."

Jeez Louise, I never knew a whisper could sound so pathetic. And Abigail thinks *I'm* dramatic.

I whip around. "Okay, okay! I went, but I hated it!" My face feels like it's boiling.

Mrs. Donnelly raps on her desk. "Lu, is that you whispering? Turn around and face the front. My goodness, you know better." A laugh ripples across the classroom.

Spider says, "Yes, Lu, you know better." Kids laugh even more, because that's how it is whenever Spider makes one of his comments, only I don't see anything funny about this one.

Mrs. Donnelly writes a grammar exercise on the board. Students raise their hands to give the answer. All of a sudden, Sam shoves a note at me. My heart thuds as I open it. *You really and truly hated it?*

I scribble an answer. *Yes, I hated it with a purple passion, okay? I'm serious. Stop asking!*

But before I get a chance to pass it back, Mrs. Donnelly's eagle eye focuses square on me, like I'm the one and only culprit. "Lu, is that a *note*?"

"Yes, ma'am."

"For heaven's sake, what's gotten into you today?" She stands over my desk, looking even more like an eagle now, one with beady eyes. "Care to share it with the class?"

Cold sweat pops out all over me. "No, ma'am."

"Well, sorry, but that's the rule. We can't have people doing whatever they please during class time. Stand up and read it aloud."

My knees are knocking like all get out, but I do as I'm told. Using as little expression as I can manage, I read it: "You really and truly hated it? Yes, I hated it with a purple passion, okay? I'm serious. Stop asking." I sound like a dadgum robot.

Everybody hoots. Then Spider jumps up and gets in Sam's face. "She hates it, boy, so you'd best quit begging her!" And the hoots grow even louder.

I don't dare look at Sam. If he's like me, he's ready to drop straight down to Calcutta, if only the ground would be kind enough to open up and swallow us.

Boy, does that ever put a chill between Sam and me. We

avoid each other all through science and math and even in the hall between classes. At lunch, he walks by with his tray and pauses at the table where I'm sitting with Abigail and Paige. We stare, his gray eyes and my brown eyes drilling back and forth. Whatever he wanted to say must've gotten stuck in his craw. Fine by me, because I doubt I'd care to hear it. Then dumb ole Lu has to go and open her trap. "Why do you even care?" I say with a snide tone. And that's when I catch something new flashing in his eyes. I can't be sure, but I think it's *hurt*.

He blinks like crazy. "I thought you were . . ." But he doesn't finish. He just hurries with his tray to another part of the lunchroom.

Different. He was going to say: *I thought you were different*. Not like those other kids who can't wait to get out of here and go to an all-white school. Not like half of Red Grove, Alabama, who shows up at a Wallace rally and waves their Confederate flags like there's no tomorrow.

"Whoa," Abigail says, interrupting her conversation with Paige. "What in holy moly was that all about?" Paige just stares at me openmouthed.

I shake my head and start fumbling with the waxed paper my sandwich is wrapped in. I see that Mamá cut the sandwich into triangles, exactly how I like it. Weird, but seeing those triangles feels like a hug from Mamá, and I sure do need a hug right now.

I thought you were different. I thought I was different, too. My eyes well up, and one little ole teardrop slides down my nose and goes splat on the waxed paper.

★34★
TWO SCOOPS

Mrs. Sampredo and I wait in the bank line for a teller to open up. Mamá volunteered me to act as a translator since she and Marina were both busy, and now I'm sweating bullets trying to figure out what to say when it's our turn.

When we get to the front, Mrs. Sampredo lays a stack of paper bills on the counter. "She'd like to deposit this money in her savings account, please," I manage.

The bank teller frowns at me. "Well, where's her passbook? Can't do anything without that." When Mrs. Sampredo digs around in her purse and pulls out a booklet, I realize she didn't need me to translate this part. Whew, because how the heck do you say *passbook* in Spanish?

The teller takes a ballpoint and writes in the pages of the booklet. Even when she hands it back to Mrs. Sampredo, she doesn't crack a smile or bother to say, "Hurry back," like folks around here do with most everybody. The marble floor of the bank lobby sends a cold shiver straight through my shoes and up to my belly. I pull on Mrs. Sampredo's arm. "¿Vamos?"

Back outside, it's a bright spring day. Birds sing their hearts out on the courthouse lawn, and the sidewalk swarms with afternoon shoppers. As we head down the block to the insurance office for Mrs. Sampredo's next errand, I keep seeing our reflection in store windows. Mrs. Sampredo is all decked out in a blue suit and high heels, and her dark hair is teased to a perfectly round ball. That shrimp in tennis shoes walking next to her? It's me. Poor Mrs. Sampredo is probably sorry she got stuck with ole Lu for a translator, and I wouldn't blame her.

At least the receptionist at the insurance office smiles aplenty. She swivels to her electric typewriter and types everything I translate. Her fingers go like drumsticks all over those keys, while I fumble and bumble my words. Then she whisks the paper out of the typewriter roller and clips it to a file. "That does it, honey bun. You're good to go now." I think she's forgotten that I'm just the neighbor kid helping out, and Mrs. Sampredo is the customer.

My brain is plumb worn out from switching between languages. "Sorry about my Spanish," I say when we're back out on the sidewalk.

"No, no, you were a big help," Mrs. Sampredo insists. "Come on, let me buy you something."

"That's okay—you don't have to!"

"But I *want* to. You need something pretty. A nice dress, maybe?"

"Gosh no! That's a lot of money! Mamá wouldn't like it."

"Tsk. Your mother needs to relax. She's always going by the rules." She takes my arm, and we stroll down the sidewalk together. "You know who I blame for this? The nuns." I can't help it—this makes me hee-haw. "Those nuns in Argentina were very strict, and your mother was too obedient."

"In Cuba, did you have nuns for teachers, too?"

"Of course. See this red mouth of mine? I got in trouble every day for wearing lipstick or chewing gum or giggling with my friends. Almost every day I had to see the principal."

"For real?" I stare at Mrs. Sampredo in her roundy-moundy hairdo, trying to picture her sitting in front of Mr. Abrams's desk, if Mr. Abrams was a nun.

She glances down at my sneakers and school jumper. "Come on. Let's find you something nice, something pretty."

Uh-oh, she's heading for Landon's. Belinda and I pinkie-swore to never set foot inside that place again! "Not that store," I blurt. "It makes me sneeze!"

"Tsk, they probably never vacuum in there."

Down the block is the five-and-dime store, which Marina claims has the biggest collection of junk she's ever seen. But she's forgetting they sell some pretty good cheap stuff. Since Mrs. Sampredo insists on buying me something, I try to decide between a tube of lip gloss and a bottle of nail polish. She makes me get both, and then we settle on stools at the lunch counter in the back of the store. I love it back here. A big mirror on the other side of the counter lets me watch customers roaming the aisles, eyeballing gazillions of trinkets crammed into nooks and crannies.

Mrs. Sampredo orders lemon-meringue pie. I ask for a double scoop of Neapolitan ice cream. It arrives in a sundae glass, topped with a pouf of whipped cream and a maraschino cherry.

Funny how one thought leads to another. The cherry reminds me of that stupid cake Abigail and I made. The cake reminds me of the cakewalk, which reminds me of Wallace, which reminds me of Sam. And he's the last person I want to think about right now—the very last. Today at school, he kept to himself all the livelong day. His gray eyes never once blinked at me. No notes. No nothing. I'm invisible again, and there's nothing to be done. *Stupid cake-walk*. How dumb of me to think it didn't matter that it was for Wallace.

Now my nose stings, and my throat feels like I swallowed a golf ball. Oh, brother, if I bust out crying, poor Mrs. Sampredo won't know what to do! So I dig my spoon into the ice cream and bring a mound of cold sweetness to my mouth, hoping the golf ball in my throat will shrink and disappear.

Mrs. Sampredo watches me, smiling. "It's good, eh?" With my tongue half freezing, I can only nod.

In the mirror, I spy a broad-shouldered lady hunched over a bin of plastic flowers. Her back is turned to us, but I do believe I recognize that shirt. Sure enough, when she turns around, it's Mrs. Underwood. I wonder if I should say hello, but a minute later, she catches sight of me and heads right over, still clutching those plastic flowers.

"Mercy me, who do we have here, feeding her face full of ice cream? If it ain't Speedy and her momma. Did you know this little girl of yours is a jackrabbit?"

Mrs. Sampredo's eyebrows shoot straight up. I jump in to explain. "Um, this isn't my mother. She's a neighbor, and she doesn't speak much English." In Spanish, I explain to Mrs. Sampredo who Mrs. Underwood is.

Mrs. Underwood looks downright amazed. "You mean you two can understand each other?"

"Yes, ma'am, sort of. I speak a little Spanish."

"I do declare, Olivera! You're full of surprises. Tell your momma, your real momma, that we need to get you in a tracksuit next year when you start seventh grade, you hear me?"

When she leaves, Mrs. Sampredo crinkles her forehead. "Did she say something about a rabbit?"

"Jackrabbit. They run fast." This just brings up more questions, so I end up explaining all about camp and the track team, and that I want to be on it—really bad.

"If you want it so bad, what are you waiting for?"

"Because I need permission from Mamá and Papá."

"And they won't give it to you?"

"I haven't asked yet," I fess up. "Mamá's been working so hard on the wedding dress and all that sometimes she gets headaches. I don't want to worry her. Plus, remember how mad they got when I ran at the club?"

"Yes, but you were running in your good dress that took your Mamá many hours to sew."

"But that's not the only thing. She thinks girls shouldn't do sports at all."

"So strict!" She shakes her fist, and I'm pretty sure she's

blaming the nuns again. "If you're good at running, nothing should hold you back." She clutches my hand. "You leave your mother to me."

I drop my spoon. "Are you saying you'll talk to her?"

She taps a long red fingernail on the counter. "Just leave her to me."

★ 35 ★
SPIDER

Spider's hall locker is two down from mine. Today when its doors swing open, bold green and red words flash all over creation: SAY IT LOUD: I'M BLACK AND I'M PROUD. They're written on a poster taped to the inside of his locker, and along with the words there's a picture of James Brown, number-one soul man, dancing across a map of Africa. I've heard that song, "Say It Loud—I'm Black and I'm Proud," on WLS-Chicago, but at the local station, Spider's not allowed to play it. His uncle says it's too radical for Red Grove. Well, if I know Mr. Abrams, this poster will be too radical for our school.

Spider and I finish at our lockers at the same time and head down the crowded hallway toward the lunchroom.

Nobody's paying us any mind, so it seems okay to ask him a question. "Hey, how come you play 'Stand!' practically every afternoon?" I have to crane my neck to talk to him because he's a good foot taller than me.

"That's just me trying to get the message out."

"To who?"

He grins. "To whoever needs to hear it."

"Oh." The hairs on my arms prickle. Does he mean *me*?

"To open their minds to what's real, dig?"

"Dig," I answer, but I'm not exactly sure what he means by *real*. If you listen to the words of "Stand!" it's all about . . . well, standing up against things that are wrong, speaking up for the truth, and not just sitting around on your duff when you know better.

"Tell the truth," he says, and I near about faint, because I just *know* he's going to grill me about the rally. "Why did you break that boy's heart?"

"What boy's heart?"

"You know, Sam, the man. You wrote him that get-lost note the other day."

"That wasn't a get-lost note. It was . . . something else." Aw, heck, I'm tied up in knots and don't know how to explain anything to Spider.

"No lie?"

"No lie."

"I could've sworn you gave him the boot, for real!"

I shake my head. "Anyway, why did you make fun of us?"

"Heyyyy, I'm sorry!" As soon as he says this, I choke up. I'm not sure why, exactly, but everything sort of piles up on me at once. I try to stop sniffling, but it's too late to hide it from Spider. "Whoa! Don't cry!" he says, jumping back like he's seen a snake, which tickles my funny bone. And now I feel silly as a goose because I'm blubbering *and* laughing. Spider doesn't know what to say to that.

Mr. Abrams is stationed at the doors to the lunchroom, like a bulldog ready to pounce on whoever walks by. Half the boys get barked at. "Tuck that shirttail in!" or "Get that hair cut!" Then he catches sight of me and Spider. Uh-oh. According to most white grown-ups, black boys like Spider aren't supposed to talk to girls like me. Wearing that bulldog face, Mr. Abrams takes one step in our direction, and in a flash, I'm Split City before he can notice that I've been crying.

A sharp left takes me to the glassed-in trophy case near the school's front doors. My heart's going like a jackhammer. We didn't break any rules, but I want Spider in the lunchroom, at his table, before I dare pass by Mr. Abrams again. For about five minutes, I pretend to be 100 percent fascinated with the trophies, which are mostly plastic goblets with tiny statues of boys doing sporty things. The only girls in the whole case are either cheerleading or baton twirling. Next year, some of those plastic girls better be running track.

In the glass, I watch reflections of kids scurrying past on their way to lunch. There go Nick and Chad and Robbie. Sam and his marching-band buddies. Belinda, with a book under her arm, next to Angie and Willa. Missy and Phyllis, in their matchy outfits. And all by her lonesome, Connie. But I see no tall boys with big Afros, so I guess the coast is clear. When Mr. Abrams starts yakking with a teacher, I zip past him, unnoticed.

Abigail says, "Finally! I was about to send out a search party." As usual, Paige is at the table, and so is Libby, a seventh-grader who's on yearbook staff with Abigail.

"Sorry to take so long. I was hiding from Mr. Abrams." I unpack my sandwich.

"What for?" Abigail says.

"He saw me walking down the hall with Spider." As soon as I notice Libby eyeing me, I realize I've said too much. "It wasn't on purpose!"

Paige says, "How do you mean, not on purpose?"

I shrug, pretending like it's no big deal. "We were at our lockers and started talking."

Libby looks disgusted. "You want your reputation ruined?"

Abigail gasps. "Lu wouldn't do anything *bad*!"

Libby purses her lips. "Well, if people see you, they'll come to certain conclusions. Plus, if you talk to those boys, they'll just take it as encouragement." She punches a straw into her juice carton and keeps staring me down.

Those boys? And encouragement for what? That's what I'm thinking, but Libby scares me, so I keep my trap shut.

In a meek voice, Paige asks Libby, "Did you know Spider is president of the math club?"

"So?" Libby scoffs. "That doesn't make him a saint. Y'all can do whatever you want, but I'm not coming back next year."

Abigail says, "You're not?"

"Nope. I'm enrolling at East Lake." She flicks crumbs off her hands in three swipes, almost like she's wiping off our whole school, kit and caboodle.

Abigail says, "Paige, are you going to East Lake, too?"

Paige shakes her head. "Mom says we're sticking it out."

"I'm not leaving," I chime in.

"Me neither," Abigail says, looking a little down in the mouth. "Daddy's dead set against it." With her fork, she pushes around what's left of her mashed potatoes.

"But you're starting to buddy up with them," Libby says to me, "so I guess you don't mind staying."

Them. I swallow hard. Belinda—is that who she means?

Libby doesn't know the half of it—that Belinda and I run together every weekend or that we talk on the phone almost every day. Should I say something? But wait: *we're foreigners—we're not supposed to get involved*. That's what's running through my head. I take a deep breath, hoping my heartbeat will slow down.

Part of me thinks, *Keep your trap shut*, but the words come out anyway. "Well, if you want to know the truth," I say, in a weird, down-inside-a-well voice, "I don't mind staying." Libby's mouth goes slack and her eyes get a hard shine that looks extra scary. To my surprise, the voice from the well keeps going. "Belinda—she's—she's one of my best friends." That's when Abigail pinches me under the table. Maybe I've said too much.

In her brightest voice, Abigail says, "Y'all, should I buy some fake nails? I sure don't want Conrad to get here and see these stubby things." She spreads her hands out for inspection.

"Jell-O's supposed to make nails grow," Libby says.

"Try unflavored gelatin," Paige says. "You dip your nails in it."

"But that'll take too long! The party's in two weeks!" Abigail prattles on about some glue-on nails she saw at the five-and-dime. "Ninety-nine cents for a pack, but the glue is extra." They go on talking about the party and glamour stuff, but I can't shake off the look on Libby's face when she said the word *them*. Belinda's not a "them." Spider's not a "them." I sure do hate it when people say things like that, and now I've made it plain. *Gulp*. What have I done?

After lunch, I find a note jammed under the door of my hall locker. *Sam?* Everything goes dizzy while I quickly unfold the paper and start reading: *Really sorry that I hurt your feelings!* For just a flash, I think it *is* from Sam. Then it says, *Listen at 4:30 and I'll play you a song. Stay cool, little sis.*

Spider, you're so nice. Why can't everybody be like you?

★36★
TINA BRIGGS

Once again, Ricky is pestering Denise. He wants her phone number. He wants to sit with her on the bus, anything. "Come on, baby, pleeeease!" The bus hasn't even arrived yet, and he's already about to give her a dadgum stroke. She shakes him off and runs to me, as if little old *me* could hide anybody from that big brute. Ricky takes ahold of both of us by our sleeves and grins like a tomcat with a newly caught mouse. "Looky here. I got me a Spanish girl, too!"

"I'm from Argentina, you ding-dong!"

"Same difference." He grabs a hunk of my hair and tugs on it till I'm forced to look at him. "You wanted proof that Tina is real, and I've got it!" I try to pull loose. My book bag drops to the sidewalk, and a ballpoint pen rolls out. Denise wallops him with her purse, but he just laughs like a maniac and keeps a grip on both of us. Somehow my foot comes down on his—hard—and he jumps back. "Owwwww!" He hops around, wincing.

Denise cackles. "She stomped the mess out of you!"

When he's done yowling, every smidgen of jokester has left his face. "You're paying for this!" he yells. The bus pulls up, and the doors pop open. Ricky pushes other kids aside and scrambles up the steps. After I find my seat, he comes barreling back down the aisle and shoves a piece of newspaper under my nose. By now, the bus has started rolling. "Don't you ever call me a liar again or I'll make you double sorry." After the way he treated me and Denise, I'm not about to look at anything he shows me. Staring straight into his eyes, I ball up the newspaper and throw it on the floor. "What did you do that for?" he screams.

Everybody quits their yakking and stares. At the same time, the driver jerks the bus to a stop. "What's going on back there?" He doesn't wait for an answer—he just orders Ricky to sit up front in the hot seat. Whew, glad to get that burly devil away from me.

When we get rolling again, I reach down for the balled-up newspaper and smooth it out. It's from the sports section of the *Montgomery Advertiser*. The part about Tina is a tiny snippet in a long column of scores and game statistics:

Tina Briggs, Upperdale, Alabama, 880 yards, 2:47.

This proves it: she's real, all right. A chill passes through me, and I lean my head on the window. Oh, brother, what have I gotten myself into?

When I get home, Mamá is hunched over the ironing board, pressing the wedding dress. The steam iron goes *hisssss* as it glides across yards of white fabric. I notice the medicine bottle on the dining room table. Oh, dear! I hope Mamá's not getting another headache. "How was school?" she asks, without looking up.

"Nothing special." I'm jittery about a gazillion things, but no point in telling her my worries. Instead, I help myself to some cookies and hustle off to my bedroom, where I snap the radio on. "Psychedelic Shack" is playing.

I spread the crumpled newspaper page out on the floor. Now where are those dad-blamed scissors? My side of the room is a mess. Right after I find them behind a stack of comic books, Ringo pops out from under the bed. He won't leave me be until I stop and pet him, even though I don't feel like it one bit. This whole day has turned me into a grouch and a half. First, there was all that stuff with Libby in the lunchroom—which I'd like to forget—and then Ricky. Yikes.

After trimming the part about Tina out of the newspaper,

I tack it to the corkboard and prop my elbows on the dresser top, face-to-face with my Olympic coach. "Madeline Manning, do you see the fix I'm in? Tina Briggs—*she's* the real thing, not me, and I've got less than three weeks to get ready for her."

Ringo jumps up on the dresser and rubs against the corkboard. "You're going to mess up my stuff, you crazy kitty." I set him down on the rug, where he starts sharpening his claws. "Stop! You're going to tear that rug to smithereens!" He gives me a hard stare, with ears laid back, like his feelings are hurt. I reach out and stroke his chin till he purrs, and before too long, I start calming down a little.

I get the big idea to take the corkboard to the living room, where everybody is bound to get a look at it. Maybe this will be my chance to explain stuff to Mamá and Papá, so they'll sign my permission slip for track camp. With any luck, Papá will see the article about Tina and want to know who she is and why I care so much. Mamá will finally notice Madeline Manning and see that there's nothing wrong with girls or women who like to run.

But no sooner do I lay the board on the coffee table than Mamá passes through with the garment bag. "Lu, what is that?"

"My corkboard. I want to show Papá something from the sports pages." I'm half wondering if Mamá will already know all about it from Mrs. Sampredo, but she doesn't give any sign of that. Instead, she slowly shakes her head, like she's figuring me for a lost cause. Maybe Mrs. Sampredo forgot her promise—or else chickened out, like I do half the time. And since Mamá is looking a little worse for wear this afternoon, I'm wishing I hadn't bothered her at all.

"Well, I'm sure your father will be interested," Mamá says with a tired voice. "He's the sports person around here. Now please get that board off the table before the wood gets scratched."

Back in my room, the minute hand on my dresser clock edges toward four thirty, when Spider's supposed to play my song. Next thing I know, the news announcer finishes up his bulletin and here comes Spider.

"Take a listen to this number, y'all. It's for a little sis who needs to know that everything's going to be cool, dig?" I smile, because when it comes to Spider, I can't help it. But the song he picked for me is "I Want You Back" by the Jackson 5—a great song, a fun song, just not one of "mine." Plus, you can't have something back if you never really had it. And for your information, Spider, I don't get the feeling Sam even *wants* me back.

★ 37 ★
RHYMING

It's Saturday morning, and Marina and I are up with the chickens. The Sampredos are coming over to eat dinner with us tonight, and Papá's asked us to help with the preparations since Mamá's been working so hard. It was Marina's idea for us to jump on the housecleaning chores right away, before Mamá could even finish her shower. The birds are still singing their morning songs when Marina takes a dust mop to the cobwebs and I tackle the kitchen counters with scouring powder.

It's pretty fun to surprise Mamá. The minute she comes out in her bathrobe and sees what we're up to, her mouth goes into an O, and then her eyes crinkle with one of those smiles that make me believe everything's going to be all right.

Papá grins and says, "Ay, chicas, you outdid yourselves!" I think Mamá may not need her medicine today.

Around two o'clock, Belinda and I meet for our run. She's a drill sergeant, and I'm her one and only soldier. "Left, left, left, right, left," she calls out in a singsong. The rhymes she makes up on these Saturday runs are getting fancier by the minute. There's one about fleas, knees, and bumblebees, but I've forgotten how it goes. One I do remember says, "Candy cane, soda pop, be-bop-a-loo. Hop, drop, stop, shop, shoo-shoo-shoo."

Today, she comes up with her best one so far: "I say lightning, you say thunder. We're the girls that make 'em wonder." I like it so much that I tell her we should make it our team cheer, if we ever get a team. Mrs. Underwood says we should know by the last week of school.

Today, we run the route at a good clip, cruising down the street under the oak trees and bouncing squirrels, and up our doozy of a heart-attack hill. Then we do it all over again. Before long, we've run up the hill so many times that it's starting to feel like we own it. Even when my legs beg me to quit, I force them to keep going. Heck, Field Day is in two and a half weeks. *Tina Briggs* is in two and a half weeks. This is no time to cut excuses.

When we finish, Belinda says, "Whew, I'm too wiped out for monkey bars."

"Me too."

"Want to go by Handy's?"

"Sure." We roll our bikes out of the bushes and coast along the street, turning into the alley and going through ruts and puddles before we pop out on Cornelius. At Handy's, we each get a box of Cracker Jacks. After running, I can't resist a snack, even though Mamá would kill me dead if she knew I was eating junk food, especially since she's slaving over the stove this very minute to make everything delicious for the Sampredos.

I get a bright idea. "Why don't you come to my house for dinner? My mom is a really good cook."

"Oh, yeah?" Belinda breaks into a big smile. "Sounds good to me, but I'd have to go home and get a shower first, because, you know . . ." She holds her nose.

"Yep, me too! And then could your mom or dad drive you to my house?"

"Probably so," she says.

We scrounge around in our pockets for dimes to call our mothers from a pay phone. The answer from both of them is *yes*. Yes! It's starting to feel like Belinda Gresham is really and truly my best friend.

★38★
GIRL TALK

We sit cross-legged on my bedroom floor, flipping through my stack of *Groovy Gal* magazines. Just like Abigail, Belinda's a lot keener on fashion stuff than I am. "Ooh, I love those shoes!" she says. "I need some of those for school next fall."

"And pantsuits?"

"And pantsuits."

She turns another page. "I love this beret! And look, it matches the skirt!" she says.

"Hey, you can take these magazines home if you want to," I tell her.

"You don't read them?"

"Not much."

"Abigail might be upset if you give them away."

I shrug. "She won't know. She hasn't been to my house in forever."

Belinda frowns. "How come?"

"She's got a boyfriend." I explain about Conrad and the WATS phone line that he and Abigail burn up for hours at a time.

"What about *your* boyfriend?" She wiggles her eyebrows. "Does *he* ever call you?"

I make a face. "If you mean Sam, he's not even speaking to me."

"What? What's gotten into that little stinker?"

I know the answer, but I'm not telling. The last thing I need is another friend getting steamed at me for going to that rally, and the more time I spend with Belinda, the sorrier I am for going.

The fashion spreads show every outfit known to man, and Belinda oohs and aahs over half of them. Then she stops at a page full of back-to-school clothes. One of the models is black and wears her hair in a cute Afro. Belinda puts a hand to her hip. "Well, how do you like that? Here's a black girl—at last. I was starting to think we were invisible."

I flip through the pages of another issue. "I see what you mean." There are hardly any black girls *anywhere*, and it dawns on me that all the *Groovy Gal* magazines are like this.

"Humph, I guess we don't get to be fashion models." She shoots me a look. "Not that I give a fig."

"Me neither. Still."

"Yeah, still." She keeps flipping pages. "My mom gets *Jet* magazine."

"What's that?"

"It's for black people, which is why we're on every single page."

"Oh. That's good." As far as I know, there's not a magazine that has people like my family on every single page. If so, there would be plenty of brown-eyed, dark-haired girls in the fashion spreads, and that sure doesn't happen in *Groovy Gal*.

Belinda reaches the cheap ads in the very back, where you can see all sorts of schools that train you for interior design, secretarial, or stewardess jobs.

"What are you going to be when you grow up?" I ask.

"My daddy wants me to be a dentist, like him." She wrinkles her nose.

"Mine thinks I should be a medical technician and work in a lab at a hospital. He says it pays pretty good money. He tried to get Marina to do it, but she has other ideas."

"Tell me about it! I have other ideas, too."

"Like what?"

"Like being a poet, maybe?" She hops up to rummage

in her purse. "Almost forgot that I brought you one of my poems." She pulls out a folded piece of notebook paper. "Do you want to read it?"

"Of course I do!" The title of the poem is "When Spring Bursts Through." Her handwriting is awfully nice, much better than mine, and the words are pretty, too, tons better than anything I could ever come up with. It's all about a yellow crocus in a dressing gown and a storm of angry raindrops.

"Do you like it?" Belinda asks shyly.

"Are you kidding me? I love it! Is this mine to keep?"

She nods, beaming. Right then, I hurry to the corkboard and tack her poem next to Madeline Manning. I step back to admire it. Yep. Belinda's poem and Madeline Manning's gold medal make a perfect pair.

★39★
TANGO

All through supper, Mamá keeps saying, "Save room for dessert," but most of us stuff ourselves anyway. When she finishes her meal, Marina excuses herself to go work at the Brewer headquarters. For the rest of us, it takes a good hour before we're ready to dig into the flan, a sweet custard with a caramel syrup drizzled all over it.

We take our bowls to the screened-in front porch, where there's a breeze and a whole lot of cicadas are buzzing in the air. Everybody congratulates Mamá on the fine cooking, and Papá salutes her for finishing the bride's veil. "Here's to good work and fine friends!"

"Hear, hear!" We all clink our spoons. In this crowd,

Spanish and English get all chopped up and mixed together, so every few sentences, I stop to translate for Belinda.

Across the street at the Mandersons' house, the outside lights flip on, and Mr. Manderson strolls out to his Chevy. "Evening!" We say hello back, and he drives off.

"You want to hear something?" Papá says. "Yesterday Manderson gave me a big lecture on why I should vote for Wallace in the runoff."

"How strange," Mr. Sampredo says. "And here you are with a daughter who works with the Brewer campaign!"

"Yes, and I'm proud of her for doing it," Papá says. "I told Manderson, with all due respect, that our state needs to go forward, not backward, and Wallace wants to take us backward."

"He is dangerous!" Mr. Sampredo says, shaking his head. "I wish Silvia and I were already citizens, so we could cast a vote for Brewer."

While they get to talking about the election, Belinda and I run to the kitchen to fetch seconds. We bring back a tray of refilled bowls and pass them around. Papá is saying, "Enough talk of politics. This is Saturday night—we should be relaxing and enjoying a laugh."

Mrs. Sampredo says, "¡Debemos bailar!"

Papá jumps to his feet. "Excellent idea, Silvia. Let's get these chairs out of the way so we can make a dance floor."

"Out here?" Mamá says. "What about the neighbors?"

"What about them? They can join us, if they like. Girls, please open the doors and turn on the stereo. We need some music."

When everything's ready, Belinda and I park ourselves on the porch swing. The sound of Argentine music pours from the speakers and flows out to the porch, where Mamá, Papá, and the Sampredos prance back and forth across the floor. The ladies stick a leg out now and then, and the men dip their wives backward. It's supposed to be an elegant tango, but it looks goofy and makes us giggle. Especially when one of Mrs. Sampredo's spiked heels breaks clean off her shoe. She lets out a yelp, and we all bust a gut laughing.

By the time Dr. Gresham pulls in front of our house to pick up Belinda, the porch is tidy again, the kitchen is scrubbed clean, and the Sampredos have gone back to their house.

Papá and Mamá walk out to the car with us to shake hands with Belinda's dad. While Belinda slides into the passenger seat, Mamá tells Dr. Gresham, "It's been such a pleasure to have your daughter with us today. She's a delight."

"Music to my ears. And it's nice to finally meet this little lady," he says, shooting me a wink. "Belinda tells me you've got a pretty fast set of wheels on you."

Wheels? I never heard anybody talk about running that way, but I like it. "Thank you."

Papá says, "We should all get together for dinner. Would you and your wife enjoy Argentine cooking?"

Dr. Gresham grins. "I would be crazy to say no to that!"

While the grown-ups chitchat about getting together, Belinda and I giggle at each other through the car window. "Now even our parents are going to be friends!" she says.

Oh boy, oh boy, oh boy. *That* makes me feel good all over.

Monday, I show Mrs. Underwood the clipping with Tina Briggs's running time. "Well, I'll be," she says, stroking her chin. "Let's figure this out, Olivera." I follow her into her office, where she punches numbers on her adding machine. "By my calculations, you're the best to go head-to-head with Briggs." She tilts her office chair back with a squeak and clasps her hands behind her head. "Think you can hold good speed for two laps? That's what we're looking at to match her time over eight hundred and eighty yards."

"Yes, ma'am. But am I the only one running against her? What about Belinda?"

"Well, now that Connie's decided not to participate, I need Belinda on the single lap and Angie on the sprints. That suit you?"

I say yes, but the idea of racing Tina all on my own makes my head feel swimmy.

She starts shuffling the papers on her desk. "And another thing. I don't recall getting a permission slip for track camp from you. If I don't get an answer before exam week, we can't include you. Do I need to talk to your folks?"

Gulp. "No, ma'am, I will."

"Good. Remember, the board of education is more likely to approve a girls' team if parents are fired up. So hop to it pronto—it's make or break time."

The moon's up in the sky, the crickets are out, and like Mrs. Underwood said, it's make or break time. Alone in the bedroom, I lay my shiny new single of "Stand!" on the portable turntable. The other day, Marina stopped off at the record store and brought it home as a surprise. She knows I like it a lot, and she's all for that, because she says it inspires gumption. Maybe she's right, but it hasn't done the job on me yet, and I've listened to it a bunch of times. I mean, a *bunch*.

When the needle drops, the first sound you hear is from those drumsticks crashing down—*boom*—like a lightning strike, followed by a long, thundery drumroll. The singer comes in right after that, hollering for everybody to stand up. I learned the words from the radio, but it took a slew of listenings to get everything scribbled down exactly right. My handwriting's not too swift, so I borrowed Marina's typewriter to make the final copy, which I pinned next to Belinda's poem.

The song says that the things I want *are* real, but I have to stand up for them or they'll never happen. I know there are lots bigger things to stand up for, but right this minute, it seems like Sly and the Family Stone can read my mind about running and how bad I want it. I put on my shoes, push myself off the floor, and go out on the porch to find Mamá and Papá.

Mamá is sitting in the rocking chair while Papá stands behind her, giving her a shoulder rub. "I need to talk with you," I tell them.

Papá's hands stop moving. "Very well. We're listening."

I clear my throat. "You know Mrs. Underwood, my gym teacher? She's trying to start a girls' track team for next year."

"Interesting," Papá says.

"Yes, sir, and . . ." I push the next words out. "She wants me to run on it."

Mamá frowns. "Why *you*?"

"She thinks I'm good."

Papá laughs. "I doubt somebody like Mrs. Underwood is an expert in such things."

"But, Papá, I've been winning nearly all the races in gym class!"

"No kidding?" He pauses and folds his arms across his chest, like this is something that takes a second to sink in. "Is this what Belinda's father meant by 'wheels' the other night?" A little grin comes on his face, and I feel a burst of hope, until I see that Mamá is nowhere close to cracking a smile.

"Oh, Lu," Mamá says, letting out a long sigh. "Doing well in gym class is certainly commendable, but it's a far cry from being on a team."

Papá nods. His grin from before is nowhere to be seen. "Your mother is right about that. It *is* a big commitment to be on a team. There would still be homework to finish, no matter how tired you were from running. We'd never stand for you falling behind in your studies."

"I wouldn't, Papá! I always get my schoolwork done."

"But what good does running do you?" Mamá says. "You can't make a future out of it. This is what no one seems to understand!" *No one?* Does this mean that even Mrs. Sampredo can't convince Mamá?

I'm getting a sinking feeling, but I can't give up — not yet. "What about the Olympics? Remember Madeline Manning, Papá?"

"Hija, only a very few people make it to the Olympics," he says. "And even when someone wins a gold medal, they still have to work a real job — on top of running."

"But people can do both, can't they?" I say.

Papá laughs, but the way Mamá shakes her head from side to side, I know for sure she doesn't see anything funny. "Lu," she says with a firm voice, "this is a distraction you don't need."

I'm dying to say, *Mamá, you don't even like running, or any kind of sports, so how could you know . . . ?* But Papá's face tells me to keep a lid on all that.

He lays a hand on my shoulder. "We don't want to discourage your dreams, Lu, but like your mother says, it's a big commitment, and we're just now hearing about it. Let's talk to Mrs. Underwood and then we can think it over during the summer."

"But . . ." My legs are trembling. "I can't be on the team next year unless I go to track camp this summer. And I have to sign up before exams."

Mamá says, "Goodness, Lu! Why in heaven's sake didn't you tell us sooner?"

"Because I . . ." I drop my eyes to the floor. "I was scared to." My throat's getting tighter and tighter as I talk. "I'm really good at running! It's what I love more than anything!" Right then, on the word *anything*, my voice goes ragged, like

I'm about to bust loose crying, which I'm trying so hard not to do. "And I was scared you'd say no."

"Hija, come here," Mamá says, and wraps me in a hug. She's quiet for a long spell while I take deep breaths, trying to keep the tears inside. Then, in a softer voice, she says, "We'll think about it, all right?"

I want to say, *Please think fast,* but I don't dare push it.

Papá says, "We'll at least talk to Mrs. Underwood to see what's involved." This is not what I want to hear, because who knows how long that'll take?

In my bedroom, I switch on the radio. Won't somebody please sing me a good song? One that says everything's going to be all right? I pace back and forth, but for five minutes, there's just one commercial after another, with loud announcers and dumb jingles. It's like the station forgot that some people are dying to hear music.

★41★
PICNIC TABLE

Lately, Marina's been at campaign headquarters pretty much nonstop. She's up to her eyeballs in voter lists—it's all hands on deck, since there's less than a week to go before the runoff. Today, my job is to deliver cookies for the volunteers. Mamá and I baked them together, and they smell like heaven.

When I arrive, some of the volunteers are passing out information leaflets to every Tom, Dick, and Harriet who ambles past the building. Behind them, Sam is up on a ladder, cleaning the plate-glass windows with a squeegee.

I watch for a second while his squeegee goes *wheeeee* across the glass. Yep, he sees me. My reflection is right in front of him, but it takes forever before he says hi. I say hi back and work up the nerve to add, "I was dumb to go."

"Huh?" he says, giving me a little frown.

"I said, I was dumb to go. You know, to the rally."

He shrugs and pushes the squeegee a little faster — *wheeee, wheeee* — across window glass that already looks squeaky clean. I wait for him to say something more, *anything*.

Silence.

There's that fish in my chest again, but it's gasping for air. If only he'd turn around, I'd explain that I shouldn't have gone in the first place, shouldn't have listened to Abigail, or written that stupid report for Miss Garrett, even if it meant getting a bad grade. My head's full of shouldn'ts, and it's too late to change a single one of them.

I go inside the campaign offices, where Marina is on phone duty. When she hangs up from a call, I sneak in a question. "Can I have a cookie?" I see how she's looking at me. "Just *one*?"

"Fine, but you've got to earn it by helping out. Take a plateful out back where some of the volunteers are setting up for a break, okay?" So when Daisy, a college girl who I've seen a few times before, grabs some cola bottles, I follow behind her with the cookies and a stack of napkins. We carry everything to a rickety picnic table in the parking lot behind the building. It's in a good shady spot to keep us from roasting in the afternoon sun. "This'll be peachy keen until the rain gets here," Daisy says. By golly, she's right. Dark clouds are building off to the west.

Mrs. Townsend, a retired schoolteacher, is already at the table. "Six days to the runoff, kiddos," she says.

Daisy groans. "Wallace is going gangbusters, but I can't imagine him winning. If he had his way, black folks like me and mine wouldn't be able to vote at all!"

"Don't you know it!" Mrs. Townsend says, taking out her pack of Lucky Strikes. "The Wallace campaign sure is fighting dirty. Governor Brewer's got to raise up his dukes and fight back."

"But he's a gentleman," Daisy protests. "He's not going to fight dirty."

"Oh, I didn't say fight dirty. But he ought to get on TV and denounce these lies the Wallace people are telling!"

If they're going to talk politics till the cows come home, I'm going to do something more interesting, like watch a caterpillar crawl up the telephone pole. It goes *galumph*, *galumph*, an inch at a time, with all that spiky hair wiggling.

Then Sam appears, drenched in sweat. Daisy pours him a big cup of fizzy cola over ice. "You ought to be inside where there's air-conditioning," she says.

He stands there, chugalugging the drink and mopping his brow. "Are you still going to the party?" he asks me. My heart goes *ziiiing*, soaring like a balloon pumped up with helium. He's talking to me! Then he says, "Do you have a gift suggestion for Phyllis?" Oh. Is that all he wants—a gift suggestion? The balloon goes *pop*.

"I'll think about it and let you know at school."

"Or you could call me." He's shading his face with his hand. I can't tell if he's blushing or blinking or anything.

"Can't." I bite my lip. "My mom—uh, I'm not allowed to call boys."

"Okay. I'll call *you* then, since I've only got a couple of days left to shop." He takes a napkin from the stack. "Can I have your number?" My pulse is a-hammering. I want him to call me—of course I do!—but what if Mamá answers the phone and it's a *boy*? She wouldn't let me out of her sight for a month of Sundays.

Mrs. Townsend and Daisy stop their chitchat to see what we're up to. I wish they wouldn't snoop on us. For one thing, they're getting the wrong idea—I can tell by their goofy grins.

While I write down my number, Sam pops a cookie in his mouth and starts chewing before it hits him that he took the last one. "Oh, no, I'm sorry. I'll go get some more!"

"If Marina will let you have any," Daisy says. "We're supposed to leave plenty for the other volunteers."

"I might have to beg," he says, and disappears inside.

As soon as he's gone, Daisy gets right to it. "That boy is sweeeeet on you!"

"No, he's not. He hardly speaks to me!"

"He just asked for your phone number!"

"Only so I could help him pick a birthday gift for another girl. For all I know, he likes *her*."

"Aw, that's just an excuse!" Daisy says. I want so bad to believe her, but if she's right, why does he ignore me when I say I'm sorry? Aw, fiddlesticks, boys confuse the dickens out of me.

"Listen," Mrs. Townsend says, "when you teach school like I did for so many years, you get a sixth sense about puppy love." She winks at me. "He likes *you*, honey."

"But he's the kind of boy who needs lots of encouragement," Daisy says. "Know what I mean? He's very shy with girls. Give him a little help."

"But I don't know a blooming thing about boys!" I figure I could've read every last word in the *Groovy Gal* magazines and it wouldn't have made a bit of difference—not with a boy like Sam.

Mrs. Townsend says, "Let me clue you in about this kid. He had to endure a lot when his daddy got in trouble for supporting civil rights. Poor Sam—he was just a little kid." She grinds her cigarette out with the heel of her shoe. "He had to grow up real fast. He may be shy, but there's steel in that backbone. You watch and see."

Daisy says, "He's a keeper. You ought not let him get away."

Humph. As if I ever had him.

About that time, everybody clams up because Sam's coming around the corner with another plate of cookies. "Sorry it took me so long," he says. "Your sister hid them."

Daisy pokes me in the ribs. "Go on. Talk to him," she whispers, but I just give her the evil eye. Sam scarfs down two cookies and guzzles another cup of cola. He wipes his chin with a napkin and says he'd better hurry with the windows before the storm gets here.

Wait. Was that the napkin he wrote my number on? Oh, brother.

★42★

GULLY WASHER

The wind whips up, and the rain comes down hard. It's what old-timers call a gully washer. Before the storm arrived, Sam got the heck out of Dodge, so now it's just me, Marina, and a few other volunteers. Since I'm supposed to earn the cookies I ate, Marina puts me to work stuffing campaign flyers into envelopes. An hour ticks by while I stuff and the volunteers yak on the phones with voters. When the rain finally slacks off, Marina announces, "Time to hit the road, Lu."

Dink, dink, dink. When we step outside, raindrops dribble off the eaves and land on our heads. We don't have an umbrella for our walk home. That's okay—the rain has nearly stopped and the sun's trying to break through. Our real problem is the water on the ground. So much of it rushes down the street that the gutter can't hold it all and it's spreading over the sidewalks, inches deep. "Better take off those leather shoes," Marina says. "We're going wading." She's wearing plastic flip-flops, so getting wet is no big deal for her.

I stick my bare feet in the stream, which is warmer than I figured. The water moves fast, and in some places it comes up to my shins. Leaves swirl by. Chewing-gum wrappers. Flower petals. "All we need is some fish nibbling on our toes," Marina says.

"Or some turtles on a log," I add.

It's pretty fun. We slosh down the first block, laughing like goofballs because it's so nutty that there's a river in the middle of Red Grove. Plus, the moving water tickles.

Marina says, "Holy moly, Lu, I can't believe your *leg* muscles! You've been running a heap of a lot, haven't you?"

"You can tell?" I stare at my legs and notice my calves bulge where they didn't use to.

Marina says, "Hang on a second." She kicks off her flip-flops. "Put these on."

"What for?"

"I don't want you to cut your feet."

"But what about *your* feet?"

"Well, I'm not running a race on Field Day."

"You remembered that I was running on Field Day? I told you about that ages ago!"

Her flip-flops are too big for me. I have to dig my toes into the plastic to keep them from floating off. Cars drive by. Although they move slowly, the waves they make are upon us before we can figure out how to escape them. I laugh my head off when Marina's skirt gets soaked.

"Ha! You should see your hair!" she says. "You look like a drowned rooster!"

I reach up to feel it. Yep, my quills are on the rise. "You mean a porcupine?"

We're almost home, giggling like a couple of goony birds, when without so much as a howdy-do, she hauls off and sloshes me with a giant wave of water. I shriek and try to leap out of the way. No such luck. Now I'm drenched. Water is inside my clothes. It's dripping off my eyelashes and trickling all over every blooming inch of me. I slosh her back. We laugh like maniacs all the way home and tromp across the backyard with squishy, drippy footsteps. Marina says, "Mamá's going to croak when she sees us."

We stop at the back steps to wring out our hair and wipe the mud off our feet.

"Hey, can you come see me on Field Day?" I ask her. "I'm supposed to run two laps around the school."

"Shoot yeah, I'll be all done with the campaign by then."

"You don't mind?"

"Of course not. You're my sister, and this is a big deal for you." She tousles my hair.

Man oh man, those words feel better than anything she could've said.

I wait till Marina and I are in the car on our way to Phyllis's party before spilling my secret, the one about boys being invited. Also, that I painted my nails on the sly and smeared just a dab of gloss on my lips. "You rebel! You daring young thing!" she teases me. But I don't tell her my biggest secret: that there's one special boy I'm hoping will be there. And that, fingers crossed, he'll be ready to be friends again.

Sam did call me about Phyllis's gift, not that it got us anywhere, except to figure out that if he bought the head-band from me it would save him and his mom a shopping trip. Since there was no sense in Mrs. McCorkle having to come by my house to pick up the headband, I offered to gift-wrap it and take it to the party. So here I sit, clutching both gifts in my lap, one of them with Sam's name on the tag and the other with mine.

I get to thinking about the fact that the headband and the purse match to a T. They're both green imitation alligator hide. Seems like Sam and I match a little, too. We both care about a lot of the same things, like music, Governor Brewer, and making friends with all kinds of kids, not just the ones we've always known. I sure hope Sam figures this out. In fact, I hope so hard for this that I think my chest might bust wide open.

When we pull into the Hartleys' driveway, I remind Marina what time the party's supposed to be over. "Okay, my study group should be done by then," she says.

Everything is nuts in the Hartleys' basement rec room. For one thing, the beanbag chairs and recliners have been pushed against the walls to clear space for a dance floor. On top of that, tons of streamers made of crepe paper hang from the ceiling, along with balloons. But the nutsiest thing is the strobe light, which Mrs. Hartley says they'll plug in as soon as the birthday girl makes her big entrance.

Paige is the only other guest already here, and she and I turn into party elves. We help Mrs. Hartley bring down platters of sandwiches and bowls of chips and dip from the kitchen, and arrange everything on a big table covered with a long cloth. Soon, the doorbell goes off and more kids stream down into the basement. Everybody chatters at once.

Connie arrives with an armload of presents, and soon the gift table is piled high. I don't see Abigail or Sam yet, but here comes Missy, with her hair teased up to a fare-thee-well. Then Phyllis appears, looking like a million bucks, with ringlets around her face like the model Cybill Shepherd in one of those CoverGirl ads. Mrs. Hartley hurries over with her Polaroid camera. She says, "Stand in front of the gift table, hon," and snaps a ton of pictures.

As soon as the stereo cranks up, the regular lights switch off and the strobe ball starts rotating. Suddenly, the room looks like a sparkly underwater scene with all the dancers swimming. The first song that slaps down on the turntable is "Mony Mony" by Tommy James and the Shondells.

It's so dark at the edges of the room that Abigail passes by without noticing me. The music's loud, so I have to yell to make myself heard. "Oh, hi!" she yells back. She's wearing white bell-bottoms and a navy top. "See my braids?" Her hairdo's a fancy twisted-and-tucked arrangement of poufy blond hair and fake braids going every which way.

"Groovy!"

"Whaaat?" She cups a hand to her ear.

"I said, *groovy!*"

"And I got my ears pierced!"

"You lucky dog!" I scream.

"And see my nails? Conrad thinks they're real!" They're glue-ons, but in this light, nobody would suspect it.

Over by the punch bowl is a crowd of boys, including Conrad, who's taller than the rest by bunches. He's got Lady Killer written all over him, down to that shock of hair that falls over his eyes. When "Sugar, Sugar" by the Archies starts up, a slew of couples rushes the dance floor.

"I love this song!" Abigail shrieks. "Get yourself over here, Conrad!" He breaks off from his admirers and takes Abigail by the hand. They swim into the strobe pool and start wiggling like fishes.

Where's Sam? I wonder. I park myself in a chair and rove the whole basement with my eyes, taking in jumping pony-tails, flashes of jewelry, and now and then, Abigail's laughing eyes. When another single drops on the turntable, the opening chords are enough to give it away as "Baby, It's You." Golly dog it, if this was my bedroom and that song was playing on the radio, you couldn't keep me still. But this is Phyllis's basement, so I move nothing but my eye muscles.

By the time "Backfield in Motion" starts, I'm feeling more and more wound up, constantly checking the door at the top of the stairs, expecting it to fly open and for Sam to come thundering down. I let myself get lost in a daydream, a really stupid one, if you must know, where he pulls out his spiral notebook and shows me a new drawing that he made. In the middle, there's a big heart with curlicues all over it, plus our initials, his and mine. All that fuss about the Wallace rally? That's history, he says, with mist in his eyes. But the door doesn't budge, and the longer I sit here by my lonesome, the clearer it gets: Sam and me, we're not really anything to each other. We're just friends that lost the friend feeling.

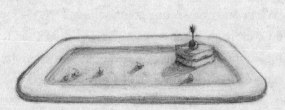

★44★
THE BACKYARD

Sitting for so long, I get a powerful craving to escape to the backyard. Too bad Jimbo and his parents have already claimed the patio. They're at the table, eating supper. Mrs. Hartley jumps up to pull out a chair. "Hey, sweetie, come join us! We may be old folks, but we don't bite."

Even out here, the bass from the stereo pounds like it's flowing through your blood. Mr. Hartley says, "You kids are going to go plumb deaf listening to that so-called music at full blast."

Jimbo's got a just-lit cigarette in his mouth. "Girl, you haven't been here in forever and a day."

"We saw each other not that long ago."

"At the rally? Shoot, that doesn't count. I'm talking about

air hockey. Nobody's challenged me to a decent game in eons. Why don't we get one going tonight?"

"You still have the air-hockey table? I didn't see it." Boy, playing air hockey with Jimbo would be way more fun than sitting on my duff for the rest of the night.

Mrs. Hartley says, "It's covered up with a tablecloth. The refreshments are sitting on it."

"Shoot, we can fix that," Jimbo says. "We'll move the food somewhere else."

"Don't you go messing with that table," Mrs. Hartley says. "Phyllis would have a duck."

"Ha, you think I'm scared of her?"

Mrs. Hartley gives Jimbo a dirty look and turns to me. "So tell me, Lu. What do your folks think about East Lake Academy? Are they coming to the open house?"

Jimbo snorts. "Mama, think what you're saying. What do they want East Lake for? They're from South America. They don't mind going to school with Negroes!" *Gulp*. Suddenly, this conversation has gotten pretty squirmy.

Mr. Hartley scowls. "You mean your daddy doesn't give a flip that his little girl has to be around them?" *Them!* My skin crawls the second I hear that.

Mrs. Hartley gives her husband a swift kick under the table. "Bob, hush. You're liable to embarrass her."

"I'm only stating facts."

Mrs. Hartley pats my hand. "Phyllis has been telling us about those high-school boys with the gigantic Afros. The way they strut around and talk about black pride, it's scary." She shivers. "I'm counting on Wallace putting everything back the way it used to be. Yes, ma'am, he's got my vote."

Right this minute, I'd give my eyeteeth for somebody to wave a wand and—*poof*—send me far, far away from this patio. I can just picture Marina at this table. She wouldn't sit here like a stump and not speak up. I mean, *really* speak up, like somebody with surefire gumption and the good sense to stand up for her friends. Me, I'm just a scaredy-cat. All I can do is scoot my chair back from the table and say: "Guess I better go inside, or Phyllis will wonder."

Jimbo calls after me, "After a while, let's play us some air hockey."

Mrs. Hartley says, "Jimbo, what did I tell you? This is Phyllis's night, not yours."

Back in the rec room, Tommy James and the Shondells are at it again. This one's "Crystal Blue Persuasion," and it's a slow-dance number. I guess Phyllis owns every album they ever cut. Just in case I missed something while I was outside, I scan every last inch of the room for Sam's long and lanky self. My gaze stops at the refreshments table. If Sam would be anywhere, it would be right here, where the snacks are. But there's nothing left to eat or drink. The punch bowl is down to the dregs, and across the tablecloth I see nothing but potato-chip crumbs. One last little bitty sandwich sits all by its sorry self on a platter.

It's no use. Sam's more than an hour late. Is he even coming?

Off in a corner, a Twister game's in progress. Abigail and Conrad are among the few still dancing. His arms are wrapped around her waist, and hers are wrapped around his neck. If this were the movies, they'd be looking at each other all moon-eyed, but he's actually watching the Twister board. Maybe Abigail likes him more than he likes her. I sure know how *that* feels.

⋆45⋆
AIR HOCKEY

Phyllis turns the music down and announces a new game, Pass the Orange, which I can tell is going to be dumb. We line up, boy-girl-boy-girl, and here's the weird part: you've got to pass an orange down the line without using your hands. You tuck it under your chin and pass it to the next kid, and the only way they can grab the orange from you is to cozy up to your neck.

There's lots of giggling as the orange makes its way down the line. Robbie passes it to me. I laugh because it's so weird to be this close to Robbie. I pass it to Chad. There's a bit of a tickle when the left side of my face mashes against his. The orange travels all the way down to Nick, who hurries back to the head of the line to start another round.

Uh-oh. Mrs. Hartley is on the prowl with the Polaroid camera. It's pointed wherever the orange goes. If Mamá sees pictures of me playing Pass the Orange with boys, I'll be grounded for the rest of the century. I manage to duck before the flashbulb goes off.

The game ends, and Abigail comes over to deliver some news. "I was upstairs just now when Sam's mother called. She told Mr. Hartley that he's got the stomach flu. I figured you should know."

Now I feel woozy and have to find a chair. This isn't going right. *At all*. Maybe Marina can pick me up early.

I go up to the kitchen to call home, but Mamá says Marina's still at study group—in other words, I'm stuck here for who knows how long. No sooner do I hang up when Paige zips past me. "She's about to open presents!"

Here we go. It's time to find out if the alligator purse will get me back into Phyllis's good graces.

We eat cake and watch the opening of gifts. When Phyllis looks at each one of the umpteen presents Connie brought and says nothing more than thanks, I feel down-right sorry for Connie. Soon, I follow Phyllis's every move as she rips the paper off my gift. She pulls the purse out of the box—that perfect, imitation-alligator-hide purse that Belinda talked me into buying and even loaned me money for—and I hold my breath. The girls all go *ahh*, but Phyllis just says, "Oh yeah, my cousin Caroline has one of these." Then she dumps it on a growing mountain of record albums, jewelry, clothes, board games, and wall posters. That gift table reminds me of the bargain bins at Landon's, except nothing's scuffed up or from the wrong season. With this haul, Phyllis could start her own department store, and if she does, I'd like to buy that purse back from her. She'll never use it.

Soon, everybody's excited about a game in the backyard. You earn points by going around on a blindfolded treasure hunt. Abigail and Conrad are first in line, and she squeezes his hand purple while Phyllis ties bandanas over their eyes. "Does everybody have a partner?" Phyllis says. I scan the crowd and see nothing but paired-up kids. Phyllis is with Nick, Missy is with Chad, Connie is with Tommy, and so on.

"Lu, looks like you won't get to play," Phyllis says.

"I don't mind. I'll just watch."

Missy says, "Too bad your boyfriend's sick."

"I don't have a boyfriend."

"Isn't Sam, son of a preacher man, your beau?"

"Noooo." If Missy thinks I'll talk about Sam with her, she can forget it.

Abigail peeks over the top of her bandana. "But you sure want him to be!" Now why did she have to go and say *that*?

"Or maybe it's Spider," Nick says with a devilish grin. "I saw you talking with him in the hall the other day."

"So? Talking to somebody doesn't make him my boyfriend!"

"Yeah, we're starting to wonder about you," Connie says. "Right, Missy?"

Phyllis interrupts. "Come on, y'all! Let's please get back to the game."

Couples run off into the darkest part of the backyard. Somebody calls out, "Watch out for dog poo!" and everybody laughs like hyenas. Not me. What Connie said burns like fire. When did *she* turn so mean? Just a few weeks ago, she blended into the woodwork, hardly paying me any mind. Does she hate me for running fast? And now, Abigail has given everybody one more reason to call me a loser.

In the patio lights, the pecan trees look eerie raising their big arms into the dark-blue sky. Moths go *bing, bing* against the lightbulbs. Abigail and Conrad stumble past with their bandanas over their eyes, laughing and bumping into each other. "I can't see a blooming thing," Abigail says.

Jeez, I feel like that leftover sandwich, all sorry-looking, stuck on the platter by itself. *Am I a loser?* I win at running all the time, so that's not it. But I might as well admit it: I'm not so hot in the gumption department. Not so hot at all.

About then Jimbo steps outside. He gets a load of all the

kids running here and yon, and of me, just standing around. "Uh-oh, looks like you got wallflower duty tonight," he says. "So how about it? Ready for some air hockey?"

Yes, I *sure* am.

Jimbo and I head down to the basement and take the mostly empty platters off the table. He tosses the tablecloth over the back of a chair. Once he flips the air-hockey motor on, we're in business. With each flick of our mallets, the puck glides over the table's slick surface. The stereo's turned down low enough that you can hear the sound of the puck going *slap, slap, whoosh, slap*. Man, I love that sound. This beats that silly blindfold game any day.

A few kids come back inside. My eyes are on the game, but when somebody near me says, "Can we play next?" I recognize the voice as Nick's.

Soon, even more kids come in from the patio, and a small crowd gathers around us. I pay them no mind. It's like I've got blinders on. I'm tuned to the same channel that plays in my head when I run: *stay smooth, stay calm*. Funny, I can practically hear our feet pounding the pavement, mine and Belinda's. Even the sound of the puck ricocheting off the walls of the table keeps time with our feet. It's like Belinda herself is right here, cheering me on. And when B. J. Thomas comes through the stereo speakers, singing "Hooked on a Feeling," a thought floods me: I'm not going to be a scaredy-cat from now on. I'm done with that. No more Loser Lu. *No more.* This feels so real that goose bumps run up and down my arms and I get a wee bit lightheaded from happiness. Even when Jimbo's the first to score and Nick lets out a big whoop, my happy feeling doesn't budge.

Hold it. Isn't Nick supposed to be Phyllis's partner in the blindfold game? What's he doing in here, watching air hockey?

Somebody starts a cheer. "Kill shot, kill shot, kill shot!" Jimbo's got a big grin on his face. With my mallet, I maneuver the puck in a holding pattern. I watch Jimbo's hands and time a hard lunge that zips right past him and into the pocket. Score! We trade off another volley of shots. The cheers grow louder.

Suddenly, there's a commotion. "Make them stop! They're ruining my party!"

Our game pauses while Jimbo yells back at Phyllis. "What's it to you if we play?"

"We had a game going outside, and now everybody's in here watching y'all!" Her face is twisted just to the edge of tears.

I tell her, "We didn't mean to upset you," but she's not listening. Her eyes are on Jimbo. Mrs. Hartley goes into a tizzy, trying to smooth things over. She and Jimbo stick what's left of the refreshments back on top of the hockey table, while Phyllis stands with hands on hips waiting for them to finish.

"Why do some people have to be such show-offs?" she says. "Some people can't *stand* not being the center of attention!"

I'm thinking she means Jimbo, but then Missy chimes in. "I told you she was getting too big for her britches—I told you!" Now kids are gawking, turning their eyes from Phyllis to Missy, and then to me. *Me.*

Along the edge of the crowd is Abigail, with her arms locked around Conrad. Her eyes are extra round and afraid. I know she can read my mind: *Abigail, help!* But Conrad whispers in her ear, and they back away into the shadows, where they flop down into a beanbag chair.

Wish I could slink off into the shadows, too, but there's no way I can ignore what Missy and Phyllis are saying. I frown at Phyllis, who's frowning at me. "When you say 'some people,' you're talking about *me*?"

Missy takes over. "If you want anybody to ever like you again, you'd better get off your high horse. Trying to be Miss Big, winning races. And hanging around with you-know-who."

When she says that, my head feels extra tight, like blood

is rushing up there from every other part of my body. "You mean Belinda Gresham?"

"Yeah. Her."

I think my eyes might be bugging out when I yell, "Why shouldn't I hang around with her? She's a lot nicer than most kids I know!"

"Then maybe you should've gone to *her* party," Connie says, her gaze flitting back toward Missy.

"Good idea!" I answer. "Since that's where my real friends are!" There's a gasp, which I think comes from Paige.

"So go where you're wanted," Missy says. "To *their* side of town."

For a few seconds, all I hear is the needle of the turntable dragging on and on, since after the last record ended, no one bothered to change it out. The silence goes deep inside and echoes through every part of me. My throat. My eyes. My lungs. My heart.

Then in a voice like a saw blade, Phyllis hollers, "Somebody put a record on already!"

I have no idea how much time passes, but centuries is what it feels like before Jimbo calls down the basement stairs to say my ride's here. I don't bother with good-byes. In the foyer, Mrs. Hartley tugs on my sleeve. "Wait a second, hon. I'll get you a pamphlet for East Lake!" But I don't wait. I tear off down the sidewalk toward the car, gulping down tears.

The sound of another Shondells number floats up from the basement windows—it's "Crimson and Clover." No doubt Abigail and Conrad are under the strobe light, hanging all over each other. Romance happens at boy-girl parties. Anyway, that's what Abigail believes.

★46★
THE CAVE

The next morning, I flip through the Red Grove phone book until I reach Sam's number, right between McCauley and McDonald. I've never called a boy before. According to Mamá, it's supposed to be a matter of life and death, and I'm pretty sure this qualifies.

About the only sound in my house is the refrigerator humming. Ringo's a tight furry thing curled up on the living room couch, Papá's out on the porch reading the Sunday paper, and Mamá and Mrs. Sampredo are on their way to Saint Stanislaus. As for Marina, she's out somewhere saving the world.

SOS. Come home, Marina. Your sister, Lu, is in need of saving. Remember last night? Remember when I got in the car after the party, crying so hard that I couldn't answer when you kept asking, "What's wrong? What happened?" I'm still sad. I feel like a chewed-up piece of gum—stepped on, smashed, and scraped off in the gutter. But I've dried my tears now, and I'm ready to tell you the whole story.

I wish I could tell *somebody* what happened. But without Marina, there's not a soul I could possibly talk to except Sam, because Belinda can never know what happened last night. And Abigail? I'm pretty sure she doesn't give a flip.

My fingers hover over the dial. It's 9:32 a.m. Have they left for church already? I dial the number super-fast, before anything can stop me. *Riiiing. Riiiing. Riiiing. Riiiing.* Twelve times and there's no answer. I picture an empty house with no Sam in it. A lonely feeling stabs me. It *is* a matter of life and death—*my* life.

Papá comes in, drops the front-page section on the coffee table, and goes to the stereo. "How about some music to liven things up around here?" He starts the record before I can answer. I'm not in the mood for anything peppy, so I plug my ears. He offers me eggs and toast, but I shake my head no. When he says, "What's the matter?" I shrug. He wouldn't understand.

Last night, I couldn't wait to get home, pull the covers over my head, and hibernate like a chipmunk all through a long, icy winter. If only I could've stayed in that cozy blanket cave for ages and somehow woken up in a different place, in a new town full of nice kids—kids who like me for who I am and don't care about skin color. But when the sun poked me in the eye this morning, I was still right here, in Red Grove, Alabama.

Siiiiiigh.

It's 10:07. The clock pendulum goes *click-click, click-click*. Ringo sleeps on. I press my face into his soft, warm fur and feel the rumble of his purring go all through me. Then Papá walks through again with a plate of cinnamon toast. "Lu, if you need to talk, I'm here." He looks worried.

I don't want to worry Papá, so I sit up. "I'll be okay." Anyway, I can *act* okay.

He hands me the toast. "At the very least, eat some breakfast."

After two bites of toast, I take a deep breath and open my schoolbooks. Exams start this week. In the morning, I'll have to drag myself into homeroom and see the faces of all my used-to-be friends. *I don't want to.* All that gumption that came over me last night during the air hockey game is gone. *Whoosh.* It must've crawled into a hole and keeled over.

Never mind all that for now. I get busy studying the periodic table. I diagram the atom six ways to Sunday and review the vocabulary list.

In the other room, I hear the phone being dialed and Papá talking quietly into the receiver.

Just as I'm putting all my school stuff away, Papá comes back to the living room. He folds his arms across his chest and says, "Lu, get up. Put on your sneakers. You've got five minutes."

"What for?"

"We're going to your school. I want to see you run." *Run?* I almost fall over. He must really be worried about me.

On the drive, Papá says, "Your sister is meeting us there."

"Why?" I ask.

He smiles. "You'll find out soon."

We drive through the quiet Sunday morning streets, past closed stores and empty sidewalks, past church parking lots crammed with cars. Something is stirring in me. I think it's that ole blue blazes. If Papá wants to see me run, I'm coming all the way out of my cave—yes siree, you'd better believe it.

⋆47⋆
SPLITS

"Ready to see this little speed demon in action?" Papá says to Marina.

"You bet your sweet bippy." She and I exchange grins. *Papá is on my side!* I think my head might go *kaboom*.

"Here's what we need to do," Papá says, pulling a small notepad out of the glove compartment. "You said that the distance around the driveway is around four hundred and forty yards, which is close to one-quarter of a mile."

I nod. "And Tina Briggs runs twice that far." On the ride over here, I told him all about Miss Third in the State and the calculations Mrs. Underwood made for Field Day.

"In other words, this race will be *two* laps around the school," he says. "Are you sure you can run twice your usual distance?"

"Me and Belinda do it all the time, up and down the streets near the playground."

"You've been running on your own? Lu, you impress me!"

I grin all over, like a puppy wagging its tail.

"But do you know how to pace yourself?" he asks.

"I know not to start off too fast."

"Smart girl," Papá says. "I suppose Tina Briggs understands about pacing."

"Seems like it, or she wouldn't be third in the state."

"Exactly. So your goal today is to learn how to pace yourself for a double lap. If you shoot for a three-minute finish, you'll give Tina a run for her money. We're going to do this the mathematical way, by timing you in splits, or fractions of the whole distance. That way, you'll know how you're doing as you go, and you can get a sense of whether to speed it up or slow it down." Boy, it sure pays to read the sports pages front to back, like Papá does every day.

"Ready?" he says.

Marina claps her hands. "Come on, Lu! You can do it!" Papá doesn't need a metal whistle. He just sticks two fingers in his mouth and lets out a sharp, high *wheeeee* that near about busts your eardrums. I start off at my usual trot. Adios, pothole; so long, teachers' lot. I'll see y'all again on the second lap.

Everything's different today. There's no Angie or Belinda

or Connie to chase. Passing the front entrance of the school, all I hear is the rope slapping on the flagpole. No marching band practicing. No baseball bats or whiny sixth-graders. It's just me and this driveway.

When I'm back in view of the chalk line, Papá is waiting, peering at his watch so he can call out my half split before I start lap two. He trots alongside me for a short distance. "Too slow," he finally says. "Can you pick it up?"

Too slow. Oh dear. If this were Field Day, Tina would be pulling ahead—maybe too far ahead for me to catch her. I rev up my racing motor and take the second lap faster. At the end, Papá says I was still behind Tina's finish by a good bit. Ugh.

But he tells me not to worry. This time, he's going to calculate everything down to quarter splits. This is where Marina's help comes in. Her job is to stand at the curb in front of the school, near the flagpole. "On the first lap, Lu's goal is to reach you in forty-five seconds. Let her know if she should speed up or slow down. On the second lap, her goal is two minutes and fifteen seconds. Start timing when you hear me whistle. Got that?"

"Got it," she says. Good thing my sister is a brain.

Papá holds off whistling till we're sure Marina has reached her spot. Then I start my third lap of the day. Those jillion hills that Belinda and I have been running? They're paying off, because my legs feel up to the job, and my heart is working hard but nowhere near giving out.

At the flagpole, Marina calls out, "Speed up a tad!" So I turn up the jets. Now the ball fields are coming up, which means I'm nearly at the half split. Papá's at the chalk line, giving me a thumbs-up. Boy, does that put a smile in my step. *Papá's helping me run!* I float like a kite on a breezy day.

On the far side of my second lap, Marina shouts, "Right on it, Lu!" But I give it a teensy bit more gas anyway, just in case. As I approach Papá at the chalk line, I see him looking at his watch, then at me, then back at his watch and back at me. When I zip across the finish, he yells, "Two fifty-eight!" That's *my* finishing time, and Papá says it's darned good.

Here comes Marina. She cuts across the schoolyard, out of breath. "Papá, what are you waiting for?" she says, collapsing on the grass. "This girl needs to run track!"

"I agree," he says.

"For real?" I shriek.

"That's right. Believe it or not, even your mother is this close to saying yes. This close." His index finger and thumb are spread maybe half an inch apart.

"Really?" I squeal.

Papá throws his head back and laughs. "Yes, and you can thank Mrs. Sampredo for that. As for me, I just needed to see your speed with my own eyes."

"Ahhhhhhhh!" I run around in a circle, with my arms spread like a bird about to take off. I whoop at the top of my lungs and circle back around to high-five Papá and Marina. They whoop with me. When Mamá gets back from church, she's going to be ready to say yes—I just know it! Wait till Mrs. Underwood finds out! I'll tell her first thing Monday. Wait till Belinda hears! I'm calling her the second we get home.

★48★
THE MIDDLE ROW

Sam's not late yet, but unless he's still sick, he'd better hurry. Homeroom bell is about to go off.

During exam week our schedule is topsy-turvy. Monday through Wednesday, we take exams in the mornings, and in the afternoons, we float from class to class, reviewing and studying. Thursday, of course, is Field Day.

Abigail's hunched over a three-ring binder, whispering definitions to herself. She has yet to say hello. Finally, at 7:54, Sam bustles in. The minute he stuffs his book bag in the cubby, he starts talking to me. "I heard about the party."

"What did you hear?"

"That it went bad for you." Paige must have been the one who told him what happened. "Nobody stuck up for you? *Nobody?*"

"Nobody."

He takes that fountain pen in his fingers and flips it over and over in a circle, like the wheels in his head are turning. *What the heck is he thinking?* I wonder. But the bell rings before I get a chance to find out.

The whole day ticks by slowly. We take our first two exams, eat lunch, and get through fifth period.

Come sixth period, I'm finally about to see what's on that boy's mind. A tall stack of review sheets sits on Miss Garrett's desk. Sam kind of messes up her lesson plans when he says, "Excuse me, Miss Garrett, there's something I need to do." She watches with startled eyes while he takes his books and lopes over to the left side of the classroom, where he plunks down in an empty desk between Spider and Angie. "I'm sitting over here from now on, if that's okay with y'all," he says to Spider.

Spider gives him a high five, then a low five and another high five. "Out of sight! Welcome to the sunny side of the street, brother!"

Miss Garret's eyes flutter in confusion. "Pardon me?"

"Sorry for the interruption," Sam answers, "but I couldn't sit in that middle row anymore. This is where I belong."

Nick mumbles something. Charles mumbles something back. Chad says, "Shut up, Charles."

In one voice, Willa and Charles say, "*You* shut up!"

Sam says to Nick and Chad, "Guys, come on. It's not a big deal—just let it be."

Miss Garrett is on her feet, looking hot and bothered. "Sam, there's a time and place for everything, and I hardly think this is the time."

"I'm not trying to start trouble."

"Oh, puh-leez," Missy says. "Get off your high horse." I guess she loves to say that.

"Yeah," Connie says. "Get off your high horse before you fall off." Missy and Phyllis shoot her with ice-cold stares.

Then Nick says, "Figures—coming from you, since you're the son of Reverend Sissy Britches and all." I expect Sam to turn redder than a boiled ham, but no, he's having a jolly old time with Spider. Maybe he didn't hear Nick.

Brrrr. Now that Sam's gone, the middle row feels frosty as the North Pole. It's just me and Abigail and Paige left here. I try hard to listen to Miss Garrett's review, but my attention keeps jumping all over the place. When I check on Abigail, sitting two seats back, she won't even look at me. Missy and Phyllis are in their corner, passing notes.

Meanwhile, Sam's at his new desk on the black side of the classroom, looking perfectly hunky-dory. And now Belinda's on the edge of her seat. She jerks her head at me in a come-here motion. She's telling me: leave the middle row and join us. But I'm scared.

For a few seconds, I lock eyes with Belinda, still scared. Hardly able to breathe, I scoop up my book bag, still scared. I hurry over to the only empty desk on that side of the classroom and claim it for my own. Out of breath, heart hammering. Scared.

When Belinda reaches over to squeeze my hand, I feel much better. But then one of the white kids calls out, "Copycat!"

"Oh, Sam!" Nick says, using a little-girl voice. "I'll follow you anywhere! *Anywhere!*" A bunch of my classmates die laughing. Did Sam hear them? I shrink down, down, down into my desk, where he can't see how embarrassed I am.

While Miss Garrett runs for the light switch, Belinda and Angie huddle around me. "Don't pay them any mind!" they whisper, but my face still burns like kingdom come.

★ 49 ★

THE DAY AFTER

In Mr. Barkley's classroom, Sam and I sit with the black kids, just like we did yesterday in social studies. I'm glad not to be a middle-rower anymore, and I'm *really* glad to be sitting with Belinda, but all morning long Nick's been calling me a copycat. Grrr. I want to spit nails! Sam tells me I should just ignore him, and I'm *trying*. I really am.

Belinda has a better idea. She comes up with a new rhyme, just to get me laughing: "Tootsie Pop, bubble gum, oink, oink, moo. Barnyard snack time, chew, chew, chew!"

But now goofy time is over. "Pencils ready," Mr. Barkley says. "Flip your exams over, and . . . start." Volcanoes, machines, atoms. The whole sixth-grade year of science ticks by in three sheets of paper, front and back.

Afterward, the room bubbles with whispers and fidgeting. Mr. Barkley puts a quick lid on it, but then Tommy has to go and launch a paper airplane. It glides across the back row, where Robbie and Spider try to snatch it out of the air. They both end up on their hands and knees, grabbing for it under Willa's desk and making all kinds of shuffling noises. That's when Mr. Barkley hits the roof. "All right, you three. I've had it. Get your things and march yourselves down to see Coach Williams. Now."

Ugh. That probably means they'll have to do fifty million push-ups, on a stopwatch, with Coach Williams frowning like a thundercloud.

While Robbie, Tommy, and Spider head for the door, Nick brays, "Take it eeeassy!" at Spider's back, and some kids snicker.

"Oh, so we have a smart aleck, do we?" Mr. Barkley says, glowering at Nick. "Get moving, buster, you're going, too."

In a huff, Nick gathers his things, but he's moving at the speed of cold ketchup. When he passes by Sam, he can't resist making a jab. "What are *you* looking at, blockhead?"

Sam shrugs. "Nothing."

"What a sissy britches."

Sam laughs. "*That* again?" I brace myself for a nasty comeback from Nick. But like the strike of a rattlesnake, Nick's fist flies out and goes *pow*, right on Sam's mouth. Just as Mr. Barkley's head jerks up from his grade book to see what in thunderation is going on, kids sitting nearby scatter like bird shot all over the room.

Blood beads up on Sam's lip. "You know what?" he says to Nick. "I don't care what you say about me, but you shouldn't—"

Slaaam! Nick's fist flies again, and they crash against a bookcase. A globe tumbles off the top shelf and starts rolling, rolling. North America, Europe, Asia, North America, bounce, bounce. Mr. Barkley leaps over desks to reach the boys. In the middle of all this, the bell rings. We're supposed to head off to our next exam, but now Mr. Barkley's blocking the door. "You're coming with me to see Coach Williams." He grabs Nick by the scruff of his shirt and calls for Sam. "You'd better come, too."

But Sam's on all fours by the bookcase. "Mr. Barkley, please," he says. "I lost a contact lens." Mr. Barkley hurries over to help him, and everybody who's been held up at the door rushes out, cheeping like biddies as they hustle down the hall. I drop to my knees by the bookcase and start searching for the dropped contact lens, too.

Sam says, "It's okay, Lu. Go take your exam."

"I don't want to."

His face is two inches from the floor, and his hand glides along in a slow swish. Drops of blood dribble on the linoleum. Mr. Barkley comes around with a flashlight, which should make the contact lens easier to spot. "Lu, this is not your affair," he says, shooing me out the door.

★50★
THE LUNCHROOM

Did you hear? Did you hear? Did you hear? The lunchroom is all abuzz. And for once, Mr. Abrams isn't guarding the door. Something must be bad wrong.

I'm sitting with Belinda and Angie when Willa dashes over, sloshing milk all over her tray of food. "There was another fight! Somebody got jumped in the boys' locker room!"

Rumors about the locker-room fight are spreading like wildfire, and it's hard to weed out facts from whoppers. Is it true that three boys ganged up on one? Did somebody really break somebody's ribs? Hearing the word *police* makes my hair stand on end. Spider's nowhere to be seen—and where's Sam, who's not with his band buddies or anywhere else in the lunchroom?

"None of the boys who got sent to Coach Williams ever came back," Willa says.

Lord, I feel dizzy, and the smell of fried catfish turns my stomach.

Mr. Barkley's the lunchroom monitor today. But with so many kids running around, swapping pieces of the story, it takes all of the teachers to herd everybody back to their tables. Even some of the kitchen ladies have come out from behind the counter to see what the fuss is all about. "You'll find out what happened soon enough!" Mr. Barkley keeps yelling.

Two girls stand on a table and holler at the white side of the room. "Y'all better not treat Spider and them wrong!" Mr. Barkley zips over and tells them to get down, then shouts for everyone to return to their seats.

And that's when Chad sprints past. "They're leaving in a police car!" Tons of us kids jump up from our tables and run toward the front entrance of the school, with Willa leading the pack. Belinda and I get as far as the door of the lunchroom before the crowd squeezes us against the wall. Elbows jab us. Feet nearly trample ours. While Mr. Barkley and the other teachers swarm out of the lunchroom screaming for everybody to get back where they belong, poor Miss Garrett trembles by the trophy case, blinking back tears. Soon, Mr. Abrams's voice comes over the intercom. "Attention. All

students return to your assigned classrooms immediately."
He has to repeat this five or six times before things begin to
settle down.

Me, I'm not even close to settled down. It feels like
ants are running all over my insides and outsides. I ask Mr.
Barkley, "Did Sam find it? His contact lens?"

"That's not the worst of his problems. He's in that
police car."

"And Spider, too? They didn't do anything!"

Tears spurt out of Belinda's eyes. She reaches up to wipe
them away, but they're flowing fast. "Don't cry! They'll be
okay!" I say this over and over, but I don't believe my own
words.

★51★
RUNOFF NIGHT

When I get home from school that afternoon, two ladies I've never seen before are standing in the living room with Mamá. Fiddlesticks. I didn't want strangers here today. I wanted to hole up with my music and play one song after another until the upset feelings from school started dying down.

But the younger of the two women is wearing the wedding dress that Mamá's been working on all these weeks, and the older one is beaming at her with so much pride that I figure she must be her mother. Both ladies have teary eyes, the kind that go together with special moments. To me, the dress was already as beautiful as a white rose, but seeing it on the bride, it's even dreamier. While she turns this way and that, sending the skirt into swishes and swirls, her mother breaks down into a happy cry.

Mamá is all smiles. "In just a couple of weeks, you'll have the bridesmaids' dresses, too."

This means more hours at the sewing machine, but it seems like Mamá doesn't mind this in the least—not when her customers are in hog heaven, and not when her hard work is about to pay off with a plane ticket.

Yep, before long, Mamá will be packing her suitcases. They'll be chock-full of gifts for the family in Argentina and stuffed with her own winter clothes, since the seasons down there are the opposite of ours. While we're up here, roasting in July, Mamá and all the relatives will be bundled up in wool sweaters. She won't care if it's cold, though, because she'll be floating with happiness. At the thought of this, something catches in my chest. It's a tiny shot of joy, and it comes just when I least expect it. Pride wells up, too, because Mamá made that beautiful dress with her own two hands—and a little help from Marina. I guess all this happy crying is contagious, because now I'm about a gnat's eyelash from blubbering all over myself.

Before supper, the phone rings. It's Belinda. All she knows about Spider is that somebody else did his radio show today. That doesn't sound good! My skin goes clammy.

"Do the police still have him?" I ask.

"I'm trying to find out."

Then she says Sam never found his contact lens and that he had to go to the emergency room with a broken collarbone! Some boy—and we're betting money it was Nick—slammed him against the lockers, and that's when his collarbone went *crack*. The only good news is that Mr. Barkley was wrong—Sam didn't get hauled off by the police after all, owing to that collarbone.

As if things weren't crummy enough, it's runoff night. Mamá and Papá and I eat supper in front of the TV, watching the returns. And what a sad supper it is. Wallace pulls ahead and stays ahead, and long before they announce it, we can tell Brewer has lost. Now I feel awful, because guess who's going to be governor again? He'd better not mess with my school. He'd better not try to send my new friends away. My stomach knots up just thinking about it.

Papá says, "Claudia, we should go to the campaign headquarters to be with Marina."

"Yes, of course," Mamá says.

We quickly clear the table and wash the dishes. It's already dark, and there's hardly any traffic in the streets. In every house we pass, you can see the glow of a TV set coming from the windows.

When we walk in, Marina jumps up to hug us. You can

tell she's about two seconds from busting out sobbing. She's not the only one. All of the volunteers are down in the mouth—Daisy, Mrs. Townsend, Reverend and Mrs. McCorkle, and bunches of people I've never met. Doughnuts aren't helping. Lemonade's not either.

Someone offers us chairs, and we join the gang huddled around the TV. When Governor Brewer gets in front of the cameras to concede the race, it's quiet as a graveyard. He congratulates Wallace on the win. He thanks voters for their support and says nothing but nice things about the volunteers who worked long hours to make Alabama sit up and notice. Mrs. Townsend reaches for her handkerchief.

It's not easy to wipe your eyes with short sleeves, I'm finding out. Somebody goes to the break room for a roll of paper towels. That roll gets smaller and smaller as it gets passed around the circle. After a while, we join hands and Reverend McCorkle closes the evening with a prayer. At the *amen*, people start swapping hugs. I get a big one from Mrs. McCorkle, who explains that Sam is home resting up from his rough day.

Marina wants to stick around to help with the cleanup, but it's late, and Papá and Mamá and I head out on Cornelius toward home. Cars roar up and down the street. Fast cars, like GTOs and souped-up jalopies. Pickup trucks, too. People hang out of windows, whooping and hollering. Fans of Wallace. A carload of teenagers zooms by and somebody screams into the night, "The South shall rise again!"

That's when Mamá pulls me closer. Papá grabs Mamá's hand and tells us to pick up the pace. We hurry past the offices of the *Red Grove Gazette*, where the lights are on. I bet the staff is at work on tomorrow's paper. I know what those headlines will be, and I, for one, don't care to see them.

The Red Grove Gazette
WALLACE WINS RUNOFF
Gov. Brewer
Concedes Race

★52★
ABIGAIL

Boy, it kind of feels like first grade all over again. Sam's missing school, and teachers will have to give him makeup exams over the summer. At least he doesn't have to put up with Wallace kids strutting around, going *nyah-nyah-nyah* at me and everybody else who supported Brewer.

That's not the worst of it. All day goes by without a word about Spider, and that's got a lot of us chewing our nails to the nub.

For our PE exam, we spread across the girls' side of the gym and use bleachers as desks. Mrs. Underwood's test questions are cinchy. Afterward, she calls Angie and Belinda and me off to the side. "Girls, I just got word that it's officially approved. We'll have a girls' track team next year!"

We burst into cheers. This news is about the only thing that could make me smile today. "And remember that tomorrow is Field Day," she adds. "Who's rarin' to go?"

"We are!" I spot Connie off by herself in one corner of the bleachers, looking at us with sad eyes.

Missy and her disciples are clustered at the other end of the bleachers, where they're passing around a paper sack. Each girl digs into the sack and fishes out a small object. I'm squinting hard, trying to figure out what it could be. Soon, one of the girls parades around showing everybody a lapel button that says WALLACE FOR GOVERNOR.

Willa snaps at her, "Hey, y'all aren't supposed to do that at school!"

This gets Mrs. Underwood's attention. Pumping her arms, she charges over to Missy. "Put that away. Politicking is against school regulations."

Missy says, "Were you for Brewer? He lost last night, in case you didn't know."

"Did you hear me?" Mrs. Underwood snaps. "I said it's against regulations."

Missy says, "You know we're not coming back next year, don't you?" She pauses. "Soooo, really, I don't think you ought to be bossing us anymore." The whole class freezes. Even Phyllis looks shocked at what Missy just said to a *teacher*.

In a dead-calm voice, Mrs. Underwood says, "Have it your way, Missy, but count on a drop in your conduct grade. And a letter from Mr. Abrams to your parents."

Missy snorts. "Ooh, I'm scared!"

Mrs. Underwood whips out her grade book. It takes a minute for everybody else to stir again. Some girls waste no time sticking their Wallace buttons on their shirt collars, like they don't give three hoots. Mrs. Underwood's spell has been broken, and they're free to do as they please.

Abigail's got a button, too, but she hasn't pinned it on her shirt yet. We still haven't talked since the party, but now I make a beeline for her. "Don't tell me you're going to wear that."

"I might." She gives me a huffy look.

"You supported Brewer!"

"So? There's nothing wrong with having a Wallace button."

"Yes, there is! Wallace is bad for Alabama. Don't you remember your father saying that?"

"Oh, Lu. Don't be a child. Wallace has good ideas, too."

"What's the matter with you? Did Conrad brainwash you or something?"

She leads me by the arm to a far corner of the gym. "Bless your heart, the party wasn't much fun for you, was it?" Her eyes are baby blue as ever, eyes I used to trust.

"I didn't think you noticed."

"Is this about being a wallflower? Next time, you should sit out games that are meant for couples. Then you won't get your feelings hurt and end up showing off with somebody's brother."

"Next time? Ha! There's not going to be a next time."

"Oh really?" Her jaw goes hard. "If that's how you want to be, I'll make double-dang sure you're not invited to any more parties."

"So you're in charge of who gets invited to parties?" I cock my head and narrow my eyes at her.

"Have a little gratitude, Lu. If it hadn't been for me pleading with Phyllis, you wouldn't have been invited to hers."

Blood rushes to my cheeks. "In that case, guess I have you to thank for the great time I had."

"No need to be sarcastic," says Abigail. "Not even *Belinda* will want to be your friend if you're all nasty like that."

"What do you mean, 'not even Belinda'? She's sweeter and smarter than anybody! You better take that back!"

Her eyes bore holes in me. "I'll take it back when I'm good and ready." With a firm grip on the Wallace button, she stabs it to her lapel. "There. Happy now?"

PRINCIPAL ABRAMS

★53★

BRAINS AND GUMPTION

Miss Garrett announces, "For the next ninety minutes, you'll have to put distractions aside and concentrate on what you've learned this year."

Man oh man, talk about distractions. This morning, we found out Mr. Abrams suspended the boys who got sent to Coach Williams. He thinks they were all involved in the locker-room fight that ended with Sam's broken collarbone, but that can't be right. Anybody that's ever been around Spider would know he *stops* fights. For Spider, just being suspended is bad enough, but it also means he'll get zeroes on his exams and get kicked out of the math club. Plus, there's a rumor going around that his uncle might decide he's too radical to be on the radio!

Willa mutters, "We've got to do something!"

"Like what?" Belinda says.

"Let me think on it."

As kids finish their exams, the stack of papers on Miss Garrett's desk grows taller. She has her red pen out, grading them. Out the window, I see dark clouds moving in. Gosh, I hope the weather's good for Field Day tomorrow. "Angry drops pound the pane"—that's from Belinda's poem about spring. One of these days, I'm going to sit in her bedroom and go through her poetry notebook, start to finish. Or better yet, spend all day with her under the cedar tree at Oakwood Cemetery, with birds nesting in the branches and butterflies dropping by for a visit.

Marina told me I should get myself a friend with brains and gumption, and by golly, I've got at least two, Sam McCorkle and Belinda Gresham.

Sam's new desk is empty now. He proved Mrs. Townsend right when she said he had a backbone made of steel. "Watch and see," she told us at the picnic table that afternoon. Sometimes shy people are pretty gutsy, deep down. Sometimes they're not, but then they put their minds to it and figure out how to grow gumption. Maybe that's starting to happen to me.

Miss Garrett is busy punching numbers into her adding machine. Now and then, she stops to write in her grade book.

Pretty soon, she'll reach "Olivera, Luisa." My final grade will be an A—I'm sure of that—but this'll come on account of my report on the stinking rally. Ugh. I didn't belong there and never should've gone. When Abigail brought it up, maybe I cared more about fun stuff than right stuff. But that was then.

Guess I'm supposed to feel a jolt of electricity or hear a drumroll in my head, like something straight off the Sly and the Family Stone record. But for me, it doesn't work like that. All I can hear is my heart, pounding like a son of a gun.

Before I can chicken out, I walk up to Miss Garrett's desk, where I let loose a lungful of air. She glances up at me. "What is it, Lu?"

"I think you shouldn't give me extra credit for my report."

"Excuse me?" Her eyebrows look like question marks.

"It's just that going to a Wallace rally wasn't a good idea. I don't feel good about getting credit for it."

Miss Garrett shakes her head. "What's happened to you lately, Lu? I gather people like your sister have been talking to you, putting all kinds of thoughts in your head?" She's not smiling. "I can omit the report from your grade, but you'd better be sure. Without that extra credit, your grade *will* drop and you may even lose your place on the honor roll."

I bite my lip. "I know, but it can't be helped." Mamá and Papá won't like it one bit when they find out I didn't make the honor roll. But I think they'll understand when I explain.

"All right. If that's the way you want it, but I must say, this is a costly mistake." When she sees that I haven't changed my mind, Miss Garrett picks up her red pen and turns to my name in her grade book. She sighs a long deep sigh that sends the daisies on her desk into flutters.

I sigh a long deep sigh that sends me floating free as a kite.

I did it. I got myself some gumption.

When the bell rings, Willa announces her plan. It could mean that we'll miss our buses, but Angie says her mom will give us all a ride home.

We knock on the door of Mr. Abrams's office. Willa charges in first, with Belinda, Angie, and me right behind her. Willa gets right to it. "Spider doesn't deserve to be suspended. He's always breaking up fights, not starting them!"

We all nod along with her. Maybe Spider did clown around with Robbie over the paper airplane, but he'd never throw fists. Never.

Mr. Abrams pushes his glasses down to the tip of his nose and eyes us like we're naughty children. Belinda seems only a little shy when she says, "Sir, if you don't believe us, please go ask the math teacher."

Angie adds, "Or Miss Garrett."

"Or just ask Sam what happened!" Willa exclaims.

Mr. Abrams harrumphs and reaches back behind a file cabinet. "Well, what do you all say about this?" Out comes a James Brown poster that I recognize, the one with SAY IT LOUD: I'M BLACK AND I'M PROUD stamped across a map of Africa, except now the poster's got torn edges and missing corners, like somebody ripped it straight off the inside of Spider's locker. "Think I was born yesterday? This is what I call stirring up trouble. We can't tolerate this kind of malarkey, now can we?"

I'm fresh from talking with Miss Garrett, so it seems like speaking up would come easy now, but I'm almost as scared as ever. With my knees going to jelly, I finally open my trap. "But that's freedom of speech, uh, Mr. Abrams, sir." In my head, I'm replaying all the stuff Marina told Papá at breakfast that day after the antiwar protests. "Um, it's why we have the First Amendment, sir." But it doesn't come out anything like when Marina says it. Biting my lip, I wonder if I made things better or worse for Spider.

Mr. Abrams rumbles and grumbles. With a voice dry as leather, he says a bunch of stuff about radicals and hippies invading his school. "Can't have that." But then he thanks us for coming in. Yes, *thanks* us. He might not mean it, but still, a teensy shot of hope races through me. Maybe Spider will get justice after all.

★54★
FIELD DAY

On the morning of Field Day, the school lawn is swarming with people. Coaches drag sports equipment from here to yon, teachers fire up concession stands, and band members practice formations. Some kids are checking racecourses and warming up for events.

Belinda and Angie and I take a light jog around the driveway, where we spy some puddles left by last night's humdinger of a rain shower. The rain washed away all traces of the chalk line, but before long, Mrs. Underwood will lay down a brand-new one, and we'll listen for the *breeeeeeee* of her whistle.

"Are you nervous?" I ask the other girls.

"Nah," Angie says.

"A little," Belinda admits.

Right this moment, Tina Briggs must be barreling down the highway toward Red Grove. The very idea gives me the heebie-jeebies, and even though Belinda says, "Shoot, Peewee, she's probably more scared of you than you are of her," I don't buy it. No way is Tina Briggs scared of *me*.

Paige comes by to wish us well, which is awfully nice of her. So far today, she's the only white sixth-grader to speak to me. She figures Sam won't show up at all, what with his arm in a sling. "He can't throw horseshoes."

"Or play the tuba," I add.

Paige says, "Can I tell you something? I left Phyllis's party right after you. I called Mother to come pick me up."

"How come?"

"All that hateful stuff made me sick. But see, everybody can't be like you and Sam."

"Like *me*?"

"Yeah, gutsy—going over to sit with the black kids."

"Gutsy, my foot! It took me forever to work up the nerve."

"So you're not mad?" Paige says.

"Not at *you*."

"At who, then? Missy?" I let that go without answering. Missy's around here somewhere. Earlier she had Phyllis and Abigail trailing behind her like a couple of puppy dogs. All three showed up for Field Day in Bobbie Brooks shirts with

Wallace buttons stuck on the lapels. I guess Abigail is going to East Lake after all.

Suddenly, Willa lets out a shriek and points. Here comes Spider, bounding across the grass, wearing a tie-dyed T-shirt and bell-bottomed jeans. A bunch of us wrap him in a bear hug, and I don't care who sees me doing it, Libby or Missy or anybody. Even Paige hugs him, and I think I might just cry about that.

"Hey, now! Don't y'all fret. They tried to suspend me, but it didn't stick," Spider says.

"But what happened?" Angie asks. "Was Nick the one who pushed Sam?"

"Yep," he says. "And yesterday, when Mr. Abrams finally paid Sam a visit, he got the whole story. That's how come me and Robbie and Tommy aren't suspended anymore." He grins. "But never mind all that mess. Y'all girls are fixing to make some folks eat dirt, and I'm here to cheer for you!"

Across the back lawn, events of every sort are underway, like chin-up contests and softball tosses. And now the teachers' wheelbarrow race is off and rolling. The Greshams are strolling all over the school grounds, checking out this race and that relay, waiting for Belinda's turn to run.

After the boys' baton relay, Angie runs her sprints, coming in second on two and winning the last one. Belinda's single-lap race is next. The Greshams hurry to the chalk line to watch, and I'm right behind them. At the start, seven girls spread across the driveway. When the whistle sounds and the rest of the pack thunders off, Belinda sticks to her game plan. She runs smooth and relaxed, like everything's under control, and like she has an Olympic coach whispering in her ear. That ponytail of hers points like an arrow saying, *Here she is, a winner!* I keep my eye on that ponytail as long as I can, till Belinda rounds the first curve and disappears behind the building. Then it's nail-biting time. As the seconds fly by, I imagine her blitzing past the flagpole, then in front of the school sign, then in sight of the ball fields and around the last bend. Finally, Dr. Gresham hollers, "Here they come!" and soon Belinda appears, arms and legs chugging like the wheels on a freight train. She's ahead of the rest by bunches. Angie and Willa and Spider and the Greshams and I jump up and down and scream like a herd of banshees. When her feet cross the line, we scream even more.

About then, a voice behind me announces, "Y'all, this is my cousin, Tina Briggs. She's third in the state." Everybody turns around and freezes, staring like she's a martian. She's not a martian; she's a tall, copper-haired girl with bangs cut so long you can't see her eyebrows. Chills run all through me. She looks fast. Way faster than anybody I've run against so far.

Of course I avoid Ricky like the ever-living plague. It's

enough that out of the corner of my eye, I can see him smirking and licking his chops at me. Also, I'm wanted else-where, because Mrs. Underwood is dying to give me a pep talk. "You've got what it takes, Olivera. She ain't got noth-ing on you. Nothing at all."

But I'm no dummy. Tina's got plenty on me. Good and plenty.

★55★
ME AND TINA

It's almost time to line up for the race when I hear Belinda yelp. "Looky who's here, Peewee!"

First thing I notice is Marina jumping up and down, calling my name. Just behind her are Mamá and Mrs. Sampredo, waving and blowing kisses. Next to Papá is a boy with his arm in a sling. He's got old-fogy glasses perched on his nose, and his lip is swollen to twice its normal size. Seeing him makes my heart go *boom*.

Papá rushes over and takes hold of my face with two hands. "Remember what you've practiced, hija. Listen for instructions from Marina and me, and you'll be fine."

"Yes, Papá, I know." Mamá and Marina and Mrs. Sampredo smother me with hugs and squeezes. As for Sam, with that swollen mouth of his, all he can manage is a goofy-sounding "Cheering for you."

It's crazy how one second you can feel all warm from hugs and smiles, and suddenly you're chilled to the bone. That's what standing next to Tina does to me. While I do my warm-ups, I catch sight of Tina's shoes. Sure-enough track shoes. And look at her legs: muscles out the wazoo. Compared to hers, mine are little ole lollipop sticks. Plus, her name's been in the paper, and what've I got in that department? Squat.

Well, not *exactly* squat. I've got Madeline Manning whispering in my ear, plus friends and family rooting for me. And six weeks' worth of practice laps on this very driveway, not to mention all the hill runs that Belinda and I have done on weekends. I'm as ready as I can be, even if my fluttery stomach hasn't gotten the message—or my legs, which haven't stopped doing the jitterbug since Tina showed up.

We approach the chalk line. On the school lawn, scads of folks are busy chucking horseshoes at pegs in the ground or sloshing water in a bucket brigade. In other words, not giving a plug nickel about this race.

Mrs. Underwood says, "On the count of three, then my whistle. Ready?" We nod.

Mrs. Underwood sends the whistle to the moon, and we're off.

Crunch, crunch, crunch. That's Tina's track shoes digging for every stride. *Slam, slam, slam*—that's my sneakers following right behind her. Pothole full of rainwater, see ya. Crabgrass patch, hasta la vista. Teachers' parking lot, catch you on the next lap. I may not have fancy track shoes, but I do know this driveway.

Tina and I hang side by side all the way through the first curve, and that's when she stomps on the gas. Oh my gosh, she can *run*! It's not Panic City yet—she's still within reach, I think. *I think*. Trouble is, I don't know how fast her gas tank empties . . . or if it ever *will* empty.

When we come up to the flagpole, Marina is at the curb, eyes on her watch, just like on Sunday. As I pass, she flashes the too-fast sign, but heck, I can't slow down—Tina's already ten strides ahead and we still have a whole lap to go after this one! Suddenly, I'm scared cold. Where are you, Madeline Manning?

After a while, the rhythm of my feet reminds me of what she's always told me. *Stay calm, stay smooth. Stay calm, stay smooth*. Her words seep into my addled brain, and I keep moving, even though my heart's going tickety-tack.

Here comes the far bend. The whole school lawn squirms with people all a-bustle. On the baseball field, they're doing a throw-and-catch relay. Balls slam into gloves. *Whack, whack*. Kids scurry around with soft drinks and hot dogs.

Teachers in their goofy shorts line up for tug-of-war. But this is all happening in the corner of my eye. I'm homed in on Tina, trying to match her, stride for stride, and doing war with the nervous bumblebees that have sprung loose in my head.

The chalk line is in view now, and Tina's still going like gangbusters. Her track shoes dig into the asphalt as she plows through the line, starting her second lap. Papá's there with his watch for the half split. He makes the slow-down sign—same as Marina did—but do they realize that Tina's never going to slow down?

Bunches of kids are cheering now: *"Ti-na, Ti-na, Ti-na, Ti-na!"* Now she turns into a rocket. Up ahead, Sam is watching from the edge of the driveway. His good arm pumps in the air and he yells, "Go, Lu!"

Mamá and Mrs. Sampredo are right behind him. "Corre, hija, corre!" Mamá hollers in a loud and husky voice that surprises the ever-living stuffing out of me.

Tina swivels her head, first at Mamá, then at me, glowering like she's about to swat a mosquito. If she's like her cousin Ricky, Spanish probably makes her want to barf.

Then—oh, Lord!—Tina steps into the pothole. *Splash, splash, kersplaaaat!* Mud travels out at bullet speed in huge drops that pelt me and everybody nearby. It's hard to say what takes her down, the edge of the pothole or its slimy bottom. She's on her knees. As I zoom past her, I hear something that sounds just like Ringo when his tail gets caught in the door. It's Tina yowling.

Somewhere nearby, Ricky is having a conniption. "Cheater! Stop that cheater!"

For a few seconds, I'm bumfuzzled. Do I keep going or turn back? But Mrs. Underwood's booming voice breaks through: "Go, Olivera, go, go, go, go!"

And then Belinda is running in the grass alongside me. "Go, Peewee! Go, Peewee!" So I do. I take that first bend, with my lungs on fire and my calf muscles threatening a charley horse. All the while, a voice I know speaks quietly in my ear: *Stay calm, stay smooth.*

Thank you, Madeline Manning. Thank you so, so much.

At the flagpole, I zip by before Marina can utter a peep. Weird. It's lots quieter on this side of the school, and I still can't hear the crunch of Tina's shoes. After a bit, I figure it might be okay to steal a backward glance because she's probably gaining on me fast. *Where* is she? I take a second peek. Nope, I can't see hide or hair of that girl.

Coming around the next bend, it's like the whole school is watching. Boys in their track clothes, girls in their cute get-ups, teachers in their Bermuda shorts—they're all crowded alongside the driveway. A handful yell, *Lu, Lu! Lu—Lu—Lu!* My school-bus buddy Denise is one of them.

Soon Mrs. Underwood comes into view. Just because I couldn't see Tina on the far side of the driveway doesn't mean she's not hard on my tail, so I keep booking it down the final stretch, burning up everything I've got left. As soon as I cross the chalk line, Belinda's wrapping me in the beariest bear hug that a skinny girl has ever given anybody. "You won! You won!" she screams in my ear.

Oh, Lord, I'm dying. My legs are giving out. My chest burns something fierce. I flop down on the grass. "Where's"— *huff, huff*—"Tina?" I gasp.

"She quit!" Belinda shouts.

"After she fell?"

"Yes!"

"Third in the state and she gave up that easy?"

Here come my family and friends. They swarm all over me, pull me to my feet, slapping my back, mussing my hair, and hollering, "You won!" I'm dizzy with happiness.

Wearing a big grin, Papá holds up his watch. "Lu, you broke your own record today!"

Then Angie leads us in our team cheer: "I say lightning, you say thunder. We're the girls that make 'em wonder!" We all go hip-hip-hooray and jump into the sky.

Tina Briggs is standing off to the side, and she's a sight. She's got flecks of mud all over her legs, and her eyes are down to slits from so much crying. I feel kind of bad. She *is* faster than I am. She is. It's just that she didn't see the pothole—didn't even know to look for it. I'd like to give her a handshake or something, but she and her mom roar off for home before I can get near.

"She should've won," I tell Mrs. Underwood and everybody else standing around.

"You're right," Papá says. "But wait till you get some experience under your belt."

"Sure shootin'," Mrs. Underwood says. "At track camp you'll learn what you're supposed to do. Next year, you'll be training and going to meets." She grins at Mamá with all the gold in her molars shining. "Holy Toledo, that little girl of yours can run like the blue blazes!"

"I know," Mamá says. "I know."

★56★
WE THREE

Papá's eyes twinkle. "We have something for the two of you." Belinda and I tag along behind him and Mamá to the car, where he opens the glove box and hands each of us a velvet jewelry bag with a silky draw cord.

We grin at each other. "One, two, three—open sesame!" Inside, we each find a golden medal strung on a blue ribbon, just the right length to dangle over our hearts.

Belinda stammers. "For me?"

"Yes, for you!" Mamá says.

We slip the ribbons over our heads. "The medals aren't real gold," Papá tells us.

"Like we care about that!" I hug both of my parents so hard I almost knock them down.

When I get a closer look, I see that our names are engraved on the medals, and so is today's date: June 4, 1970. I can tell that Papá did the engraving. Mamá threaded the ribbon through the loops at the top of each golden disk, securing them with tiny, perfect stitches. "You can keep that medal your whole life," Papá says. "But pretty soon, you'll have lots of others."

Belinda's parents had to go home after her race, Papá is in a hurry to get back to the store, and Mamá needs to tend to the bridesmaids' dresses. Papá tosses our car keys to Marina. "We're riding with Mrs. Sampredo. Can you get Sam and Belinda home?"

We pile into the car. From the front seat, Marina says, "So, Lu, who's that gold medalist you like so much?"

"Madeline Manning."

"Sometime I want you to explain why she's so special to you."

Belinda digs an elbow in my side and giggles. "She's Lu's coach."

Marina doesn't have the foggiest idea what Belinda is giggling about. "You girls are going to get a taste of real track coaching pretty soon."

Real track coaching. I'm ready. I'm chomping-at-the-bit ready. Monday before daybreak, we'll board a bus for our first track camp. Between now and then, I've got to label everything. *Lu Olivera* on my bedsheets. *Lu Olivera* on my bedroll. *Lu Olivera* on my towels, T-shirts, socks, and everything I take with me.

We join a stream of cars and buses leaving the school. It's weird not being on Bus 18, inching around the curves of the driveway and bumping over the pothole. Man oh man, I love that pothole now. It saved my run against Tina, and I sort of hope the school never fills it in.

About the time we pull out into the street, something happens. Sam's free hand slides next to mine and our pinkies touch. Did he do it on purpose? I cut my eyes over and can't tell because he's looking off in another direction. Belinda's too busy smiling at her medal to be of any help, and then—holy smoke!—Sam's whole hand edges over, and his fingers curl around mine. *Bumblebees, weak in the knees!* Belinda may not notice our hands, but I bet she hears my heart going ninety to nothing. I don't want Marina to notice, so I clamp my smile shut and look dead ahead at the dashboard. There's not much I can do about my face turning bright pink, though.

Sam says, "After track camp, can y'all go bowling?"

Somehow, I get my mouth to work. "You'll have to teach me because I don't know how."

When Belinda finally gets a quick look at our hands, what does she do? Dies laughing. Normally, this would get my goat, but with my hand inside of Sam's, it's kind of hard to get worked up about anything.

"Dang it!" Sam says. "My collarbone. I can't bowl—not for six weeks. What else can we do for fun over the summer?"

"How about meeting at the playground?" Belinda says. "You could swing, one-armed."

"Yeah. And when is one of those international things y'all go to?" he asks me.

"Not till October."

"Shoot, that's a long time from now."

Belinda says, "Let's have a party at my house and invite all our friends!" This gets us chattering like chipmunks. We have plenty of ideas about who to invite and how to decorate.

"I saw a strobe light once, and it was pretty cool," I tell them.

"Neat-o!" Belinda says. "And Spider has a humongous stack of records he could bring." Sam wants to know what kind of records, and Belinda rattles off a dozen names.

Now I chime in. "Hey, Sam, remember when you asked me what kind of music I like? I have a new favorite band now—Sly and the Family Stone—but the song I'm really crazy about is by Van Morrison. I've been meaning to tell you that."

"Is it 'Brown Eyed Girl'?" he says. "I love that song."

"You *do*?"

"Oh yeah."

"How come?"

He blinks about a million blinks, then drops his voice to a whisper. "Because *you've* got brown eyes." He smiles, but with that busted-up lip, it's a crooked, halfway-sad-looking smile.

"I didn't think you noticed my eyes," I whisper back.

"Sure, I did—a long time ago."

Boy oh boy, the way thunderbolts are going off in my head, I have to sit back and get ahold of myself. And guess what? It just now hits me that behind his glasses, his eyes look as tiny as BBs, like before he got contact lenses, like before I started catching on that he's a real boy, with realness all through him. He may be back to old-fogy glasses for a while, but ask me if I care. And anyway, I don't look so hot myself right now. I'm sweaty and stinky and splattered with mud, and my hair must look a fright. Sam doesn't seem to mind any of that.

He noticed my brown eyes. Golly Moses, he *really* noticed them.

Yeah, this is a pretty good day.

AUTHOR'S NOTE

★ ★ ★

Although Red Grove, Alabama, is imaginary, and so are the characters who populate it, certain people in this story existed in real life.

George Wallace served his first term as governor of Alabama from 1963 to 1967. He was known for his strong segregationist policies, in particular his attempts to block black students and white students from attending school together. Wallace's wife was governor after him, with Albert Brewer serving as her lieutenant governor. When she died in office, Brewer took over as governor of Alabama.

In 1970, Albert Brewer and George Wallace went head-to-head against each other in the primary election for their party's nomination. Wallace ran a particularly nasty campaign, relying on racist rhetoric and personal attacks to defeat Brewer. To accurately convey the cultural milieu of this election, I dug through old newspaper articles and consulted the work of historians. My research helped me craft a fictional political rally that stayed true to the tone and message of stump speeches Wallace delivered during this campaign.

While a cakewalk has become a common carnival game, cakewalks have a complicated and troubling history. They originated on antebellum plantations and were later incorporated into vaudeville and minstrel shows, often performed by white actors in blackface.

Madeline Manning may have served as Lu's imaginary running coach, but she was also a true American sports hero. She won many national titles and competed in three Olympic Games, including the 1968 Olympics in Mexico City where she won a gold medal in the women's eight-hundred-meter race.

The war in Vietnam was in full swing during Lu's childhood, and like Marina, many college students objected to the U.S. involvement in the conflict. There were numerous antiwar protests, including one that resulted in the tragic shooting of student protestors at Kent State University in Ohio.

Researching historical details is an important part of an author's job, and luckily for me, I love history. But some aspects of this story didn't require much research. I lived them.

I remember televisions with antennae and telephones with rotary dials.

Just as Lu did, I spent time flipping through magazines for young girls, which, like the fictional *Groovy Gal*, overwhelmingly featured white models.

Pop radio filled the background of my youth, and I can still hum along with many of the hits from those years. The song titles and recording artists mentioned in this story—including Van Morrison, James Brown, and Sly and the Family Stone—are real.

Finally, like Lu, I immigrated from Argentina to the United States at a young age and grew up in a small town in central Alabama that closely resembles Red Grove. I vividly recall the academic year of 1969–1970 as the moment when public schools in my district desegregated. These recollections remain sharp in my mind and informed Lu's story, both in the events portrayed and in the emotions the characters experience.

ACKNOWLEDGMENTS

★ ★ ★

So many good people have poured heart and soul into helping this story become a reality. I want to publicly recognize a notable few with my thanks:

To my agent, Adriana Dominguez, who pumped me with sage advice and steady encouragement, and who traveled the journey from rough draft to finished novel by my side.

To Eileen Robinson, whose expert eye and nurturing manner infused me with fresh energy at a timely moment.

To Andrea Tompa, who answers to my idea of a dream editor, and whose kind and thoughtful feedback have proved invaluable.

To Kharissia Pettus, for her warm and wise input on vital topics.

To Maryellen Hanley, in whose able hands I landed and found spot-on art direction.

To Tanya McKinnon, for sharpening my vision and urging me to reach higher.

To Matt Roeser, who's responsible for numerous iconic Candlewick covers and who struck gold again in the design for *My Year in the Middle*.

To my husband, Paul Weaver, who offered encyclopedic knowledge on running and the sport of track and field, and who is also my most ardent cheerleader in writing and in life.

To friends, family members, and colleagues who have believed in me, including my children: Jude, Ben, and Caitlin. Your support continues to make all the difference.

LILA QUINTERO WEAVER was born in Argentina but grew up in Alabama, where she still lives with her husband. She is the author-illustrator of *Darkroom*, a graphic memoir. *My Year in the Middle* is her first book for young readers.